To Vinette from Ray

To mi big fren, Still on vacation one more

The Silent Hurt
of
Charolette Erica Atwell

Thanks for your support

Ranston Ray Foster

Written by Ranston Ray Foster 2015

All characters in the story are fictional. Any resemblance to actual persons, living or dead is purely coincidental.

The Silent Hurt of Charolette Erica Atwell is purely a work of fiction and is in no way autobiographical.

ISBN:1522894225

ISBN:13:9781522894223

Table of Contents

Acknowledgments

I have met some wonderful people on my journey:

Rev. Dr. Kirkpatrick Cohall, my pastor and mentor, continue to preach God's word with the clarity and undiluted gospel of Jesus Christ. Min. Sophia Cohall, Rev. Dr. Sharon Downer, Dr. Tamara Henry, Rev. Dr Melrose Rattray, who has been a source of sound reasoning and guidance; love her to pieces. Rev. Adam Pryce, thank you for your support and encouragement. Thomas Kidd, what can I say about Bro. Kidd? When I was at my lowest point, he blessed me in ways that only God himself could have. I am forever grateful. Ann Marie Karlene Goddard Foster, thank you for helping me out of my situation 22 years ago. Maya Rayann Foster and Myles Foster, your kind words of encouragement mean a lot and keep me going at all times. I love you both. Omaine Ray Foster, you are an amazing kid. I ask for your forgiveness. I know I wasn't there to experience a lot of things but I will make it up to you. Ramone Ranston Foster, I owe you a lot. Sorry for the years I missed out on seeing you grow up to be that smart intelligent young man. Your mother Marcia Smith, one phenomenal woman; there is no other woman who could have been your mother. Carmen Kinkead, Colleen Faulknor, Keisha Latoya Lewis, my HNC. Gregory Atwater still working on my strengths and weaknesses; you're one of the smartest individuals I know. Thank you for believing in me and allowing me to realize some un-tapped potential. To two of the greatest friends ever, Donavan Nelson, and Richard Anderson; good to know when you're at the point of desperation and despair you have friends like you both. "One love." Donna Logan, Audrey Lewis, Austin Lewis, Christopher Dunn, Basil Lawes, Bentley Gayle, Ruel Wallace, Dr. Nathan Duncan, and all my Lenox Road Baptist Church Choir Members. To all the Teen Boys and Teen Girls I've taught Sunday School for the last 12years; you've made me so proud to see you all grew up to be successful and still in the presence of God.

The Silent Hurt of Charolette Erica Atwell

Introduction

It's funny how much you can recall in only a moment. It had been a while since I had thought about the tropical island I had grown up in with its lush green trees, endless white sand beaches, flowing rivers that invited every boy to jump in for a splash, and its bright, almost too bright, sun rising above the mountains in the east to begin its daylong reign. As I began packing my bags for my return, I realized how much time had passed since those days of innocence. Charolette Erica Atwell. Her life had not been an easy one; but I did not know that then until much later. She had borne her hurts with so much strength and resiliency, and the lessons she had learned had served her well; they had also served me well.

The plane touched down with a bump and the passengers cheered and applauded. What a way to welcome a man home. My heart had a heaviness that had been my companion since the news had come. I glanced through the airplane window and watched the tarmac roll by amid the roar of the engines. Then there was a silence as the plane taxied to the gate. Uniformed men and women moved soundlessly as they busied themselves with their business. The sounds of seatbelts clicking to their unlocked position wakened me from my reverie and I looked around at my fellow passengers rising to make a quick exit.

I am finally home, I thought as I walked free from the hassle of Customs and Immigration and outside to where the tropical sun helped me recall memories of a time long past.

The Silent Hurt of Charolette Erica Atwell

My Early Years with Charolette Erica Atwell

I awoke early to the sounds of the roosters making their famous wake up call. In the distance, a donkey brayed and I could hear the coo of the pigeons from next door. I stretched as I yawned and looked back to where my siblings were also rising to meet the day. It was almost as if I had gone back in time and we were children again, all four of us, lazy to begin the day, but anxious and excited about what was to come.

We were this great big family that lived our lives within the confines of our humble dwelling. Most mornings the neighbors would pass by and call out to either of my parents just to say "Good morning!" or "How are you doing?" Then the conversation would begin about the children and how they were doing in school. I was always amazed by some of the conversations I sometimes overheard. Not that I was eavesdropping; but, eventually you would hear about the new challenges and obstacles they were all facing with children and jobs and spouses and everything else that was their life. Although it was not always bad. Sometimes there would be good news of births or unexpected achievements and discoveries.

The thought of a new day brought such joy, peace, and sometimes a whole lot of bickering between each of us as siblings: who uses the bathroom first, who gets to iron their clothes first, that is how the mornings usually transpired. Mother would be in the kitchen cooking or making breakfast and you could smell that sweet aroma of the good old island spice.

Our meal was planned for each day. Mother would cook up a storm, to put it lightly. We were sure of Chicken Foot Soup, Red Peas or Beef Soup on Saturdays.

I could hear mother in the kitchen as she stood there cooking and singing her favorite songs, her voice a sweet soprano. Sometimes her tired body ached to a level of discomfort, which, as a child, I could see but could never understand. At no time did I hear her complain or murmur about what she was doing.

Her concept of family was pretty straightforward: we sit together and eat; even if it's only a slice of bread, it is significant that we eat together as a family. Some of the most memorable times were sitting in the wooden kitchen on whatever there was to sit on listening to the stories she shared of what life was like in her youth. The funny thing about those beautiful moments is that we never really had the audacity to even question what was for dinner. We were just grateful for the meal. Then again, it's not like we had a choice.

Mother, Charolette Erica Atwell, was committed to her family, making sure they ate a delicious meal at every stage of her daily chores. Now, as a part of the process in all the sweet aroma circulating around the air, my role was to make sure we had water at all times to wash the pots, pans, and utensils.

I would get up early in the morning to go to the standpipe with a white bucket to fill with water to fill the drums that were located at specific location in the small space of the yard. All of this had to be done before going to school in the morning. Making sure water was there for mother to cook, I never complained or grumbled about fetching water for the good of all of us.

There was so much to appreciate growing up on this paradise island that it was hard to imagine being anywhere else. The beauty of the whole family being in one small house sharing and caring with absolutely no animosity in terms of just being there for each other and sharing everything was just amazing.

We rose from our slumber early in the morning to start our chores, whether to get water to fill the drums or taking the cattle out to the fields. At that early age, we were taught the value of work ethics with regards to doing the simple things that were required of us. Each day was a new challenge for us in conforming to our parents' expectations and rule and regulations and, I must tell you, it was a lot. At times we didn't even understand the significance of the many island parables like "Children must be seen and not be heard" and I mean not heard.

The truth of the matter is, we were disciplined enough not to even try to comprehend the meaning, just know you never get into conversation that parents are having. Though at the time that was a little ridiculous; but who am I to even mention that I oppose such one-sided dictatorship, if you will?

Those experiences taught me the value as a child to have the utmost respect for my parents and those who are older in the sense of interrupting when conversation does not include me or my siblings. "Speak when you are spoken to; answer when you are called!"

The Silent Hurt of Charolette Erica Atwell

But, with all of that being said, who was Charolette Erica Atwell?

Charolette Erica Atwell had this sweet, kind spirit about her that involved such a broad sector of her surroundings. Everyone who came in her presence was always in awe of her demeanor and generosity. What I've learned from her is that kindness is contagious and should be a part of everyone's daily life. There is nothing too hard or difficult for her to do in assisting her neighbors; it comes so naturally to her. I never understood how she made it look so simple and   effortless.

Whenever she cooked, she made sure that at least two or three extra plates were set aside just for anyone who passed by and needed something to eat. And I can tell you with a degree of certainty that each time someone showed up, they *would* have something to eat.

I've always thought of her in terms of cooking and leaving food for people she didn't even know. It was an act of kindness that never fazed her in any shape or form. Providing food for strangers was never a subject that was discussed in a way that would allow someone to feel unwelcome. Although we never had much, the joy and satisfaction on her face when she could feed one more person was priceless.

Seeing such commitment from my mother taught me a whole lot about humility in the sense that kindness is a great and rewarding experience, helping when there is a need. She would give you a whole lot of insight on the importance of giving and sharing while justifying the reasons she had done such kindness as "Biblical Principles and it is the right thing to do." I've seen people from every

The Silent Hurt of Charolette Erica Atwell

sector of the community come and sit and eat as if they were a part of the family as they conversed about the children in the community, how they are doing with their school work and so on. After everyone finished eating and their stomach was full with the delicious spicy and sweet meal that was cooked by hands of love, the hard work would begin to clean up the kitchen.

Standing on those tired feet, humming the hymns of the church in this beautiful soprano voice which would just resonate through the air and flow with such a sweet and calming aura, Mother bore her burdens with faith. Scouring those huge pots and pans, and I'm telling you, they were huge and kind of heavy; not like these nowadays made of light iron or metal. I think most of the time it gave her more satisfaction seeing her family had something to eat and also she was able to provide for someone else.

Seeing her with such committed work ethics to her family, friends, and strangers was troubling to me. I was always wondering why she would extend her tired body trying to please everyone else. At that tender age I could see through the barrier that she had built up for many years, hiding the long suffering and pain. No matter what her reasons were, I never got the logic of why she would push her tired body to the limit.

After she was done washing and cleaning up the utensils, you could clearly see the through the burden of a tired soul. Mother would take off her shoes and hoist her tired feet on one of the wooden stumps in the kitchen that we used as a stool. Charolette would just sit there and you could see just by the look on her face that her thoughts and dreams were running far away.

The Silent Hurt of Charolette Erica Atwell

"Mother, its bedtime," I would remind her.

"The pots and pans need to be washed," she reminded me in the midst of her exhaustion. "We can't have dirty pots and pans left over night."

Dutifully, I completed my chore. After everything was finished washing and cleaning, it was usually very late at night. The shadows cast on the wall by the light of a bottle torch fueled by kerosene oil with a wick made out of paper or cloth, the thick black smoke moving around in the wooden kitchen, were somehow comforting. Charolette had given her all that day; the sweat and commitment were sincere and undeniably a sacrifice she made willingly without a murmur. It was undoubtedly both amazing and painful to watch.

For Charolette Erica Atwell, education was an important part of a child's life. School was a place where learning was a key fundamental in the process of educational achievement. We didn't have a choice but to go and learn to the best of our ability. We also had a lot of fun playing soccer, cricket, track and field, swimming, and tree climbing.

The beauty of the whole family being in one small house sharing and caring with absolutely no animosity in terms of just being there for each other and sharing everything was just amazing. We rose from our slumber early in the morning to start our chores, whether to get water to fill the drums (me), or taking the cattle out to the fields. At that early age, we were taught the value of work ethics with regard to doing the simple things that were required of us. It was a wonderful time just doing the things that normal kids do.

The Silent Hurt of Charolette Erica Atwell

During our summer break my parents would send my sister and I to the country where our uncle lived. I think this is one of the things my sister and I never really looked forward to doing for the simple fact that the country was dark and lonely. There was no excitement like living in the city where the lights, buses, cars, trucks and everything are more accessible.

But, things were going to change for us. I was still a youngster when my mother migrated to Canada for a better life. But there were other changes that occurred before that; life as we knew it would never be the same.

Growing up was always a fun time for me and my siblings. Going to the beach, the river, and playing in the sun all day was just a normal day for all of us. Before my mother migrated, the love and generosity towards their children was just a great example of parenting.

The funny thing I must say is, we didn't even know we were poor in the sense of never seeing or hearing my parents complain about not having the means to feed us. My brothers and sisters were always together in some of the most difficult days being a family. Even in her time of what I considered to be extreme hardship, I was truly blessed and fortunate to experience the courage of a mother's love for her family. She had this love and passion for the needs and the future of children of the small community of this beautiful tropical island. I knew the whole concept of what it means to have little or nothing. I grew up seeing my mother always working extremely hard, trying her best to make ends meet to provide for her family.

The Silent Hurt of Charolette Erica Atwell

My dad, George Washington Atwell, was a quiet soul who never talked a lot, but was such a tower of strength to her in many ways. Dad would get up early in the morning for work with a sometimes stoic demeanor. Not saying much, he would remind us about the goodness of having both parents to guide and take care of us, and that we must not take it for granted.

I remember sitting up at nights until the wee hours of the morning assisting mother with lining plastic bags for her to take to the market for sale in the capital city. Some of my fondest memories are standing downtown in the capital at a specific location selling the bags to people who came to market and needed the bags to put their items in. At times, it was pretty exhausting because of the extremely hot sunny days that I would always try to find a cool shade to sit or stand with juice purchased from vendors pushing a handcart with sheared ice and syrup.

After that break, I would continue along in my youth and innocence shouting "Plastic bags!" Those days there were a lot of young boys hustling and selling all kinds of items and souvenirs. We were all trying to do, basically, the same thing: trying to help our mothers in any way that we could. What made it so special was that there were a lot of people from all walks of life who had come to the capital for shopping and purchasing what they needed. I would sell most of the day before nightfall and would go back to mother and give her the money that was earned during the day.

I can't really express the feelings or joy, if you may, that it brings within me. I knew deep within my heart I was helping my mother and that was the most significant thing at that time in my youthful years. The funny thing about

The Silent Hurt of Charolette Erica Atwell

all of the effort that I put in, and I'm telling you, it is a lot of work, I would go back to my mother and the same thing that she was saying in the morning was always the same thing she was saying in the evening:

"Lord, it tough out here. I can't make a penny."

On the other hand, she would be saying:

"The little money I made is just to buy food and you school uniform."

We would stay all day trying to make every penny that was there to be made. Mother and I would be getting ready to go home, but first there would be some shopping to do for ourselves such as buying bread, cabbage, and codfish for Sunday morning breakfast, and school items and other necessary items we would need to sustain us. Now when it was time for us to go home, my mother and I would take the bus. That is where you heard some of the most comical stories and crazy ideas in the sense of just bragging about everything. You know deep down they were just stretching the stories.

I would just stand in the bus and listen. The reason for that is not as if I could sit while there were women on the bus; it was mandatory to allow our parents, especially the females, to sit. The fragrance of all the hot bread, fruits, and meat would saturate the bus. On reaching our stop, we would have to be stepping over bags and baskets in the bus, maneuvering our way out of the bus. One of the highlights was seeing all these kids waiting at the bust stop for their parents in order to assist them with the bags home.

I vividly remember when we got off the bus, there was a bar right at the corner. Most of our dads were inside there talking and telling some serious stories and I mean stories. I could hear all kind of arguments: who was the best cricketer, domino player, soccer player, and just a whole lot of other stuff that I can't even imagine being like that. As a young boy, seeing and hearing all the crap from these men, including my father sometimes, my thoughts tended to run wild. Mother would pinch my ears and bring me back to reality with a stern warning:

"Ah hope you don't become like these old fart yah."

The funny thing about this was that my dad was a part of the group. I guess she never really cared for all the years of hearing the same old stories. I guess she concluded that he would never change; he and his friends will be saying the same things for a very long time.

As a young boy, I can remember quite vividly how she had found a way to cover her tiredness and hide it from me. I was always in the kitchen with her, helping her the best possible way I could. Most of the time we would converse about what I would be wearing to church the next day or the day's activities with regards what had taken place at the market. It wasn't really much to talk about, but I think I was just a source of conversation during those times of her thought process. When she finished cooking for the family, which included George my dad, brother Jacob, and sisters Sandra, and Olivia, I would sit on the piece of stump inside the wooden kitchen and eat with her. I couldn't help sometimes but to allow her to doze off into that pleasant sleep which she took after her tired body had reached the breaking point. After a while, I would gently tap her and remind to her in a loving kind way, "mom, is time for bed."

The Silent Hurt of Charolette Erica Atwell

Can you imagine the overwhelming feelings and in one sense the satisfaction of seeing her family having gone through another day with something to eat? Even after all that commitment and hard work she would still be concerned about the pots and pans being put away. She didn't want to leave anything unwashed for the fear of rats, roaches, and other things that might draw attention to dirty utensils.

Charolette would remind me to go and brush my teeth and wash my face then say my prayers, which was of great importance, thanking God for another day. Even in her time of what I considered hardship, I am truly blessed and fortunate to have experienced a perfect example of a great individual Charolette Erica Atwell who has been an inspiration to everything I do in terms of my action(s) with regards to kindness.

When she had blown out that light with the lampshade that had the words "Home Sweet Home" for that night to take that well deserved rest in sweet dreams, from the heavy lifting of taking care of her family; that was when her day actually ended.

The Life of Charolette Erica Atwell

Charolette Erica Atwell was born to Philip Elliott and his wife Helen Rowe in the rural part of the island, a very remote part of a scenic paradise. It was a tiny rural community where trees, rivers and mountains were visible all around; the scenic views were just awesome.

Philip Elliott was a tall man who always rode a lily white horse; everybody in the community knew who he was. His wife Helen Rowe was born to descendants of former slave owners; she had this long, beautiful hair and she was small in stature.

Charolette was a treasured child, although her earliest re-collection of her childhood was sometimes blurred by the difficulties of minimal access to the outside world because she had never been outside of the community. She never knew what it was like to experience the more developed areas of the island. Charolette would remind my sisters and me about some of the difficulties she experienced. You would hear the cracking of her voice as she tried to articulate everything that was hard and painful.

I guess the same upbringing that she had was instilled in my siblings and I, like waking up early in the morning, taking the animals out in the fields, fetching water, and sweeping the yard before school. She explained, without uncertainty, the luxury we were enjoying now. She didn't have such luck; therefore, we must be grateful.

The Silent Hurt of Charolette Erica Atwell

School was a priority whether she liked it or not. It was most daunting doing all of those chores then dress for school and walk about two miles to school each day. Talking about school was so heart wrenching seeing how hard it was; but, she learned to accept and adapt to the norm at that point in her life. So, whenever we talked about school with her, then you would hear the long lecture on the importance of school and its reward and the benefits of getting a good education.

I knew it had to be extremely hard for her shouldering such a burden as a child in her tender years. I don't think she was trying to live her dreams through her children but, the thought of her children struggling and going through such serious challenges was not an option in her book. As she eloquently spoke about the importance of school, you could see the passion in her breathtaking brown eyes and slender frame. Through all of the challenges in her early childhood, her manner toward her parents never wavered nor did she blame them for any of the challenges she experienced.

Honoring your parents was taught at an early age, which is biblical principles as one of the promises God made to his people so that days may be long and to enjoy the peace of God. Charolette never really elaborated much on her schooling or on how much she had excelled in terms of her academics. All I know is that she was brilliant in conversation with anyone on any topic that was relevant or of importance to her.

A lot of her childhood growing up was centered on her parents' expectations and decisions for her. It was very hard to fathom even when she tried to explain the significance of obeying her parents' expectation of her. Her days were spent doing what I guess was her commitment to her parent's every instructions. My thought process at that time during the conversation, and must I say strict reminder, disobeying your parents was not an option, then I was sternly reminded about the behavior of the current group of children. Note: (Imagine if she was dealing with the current group of the children in this age of technology; not sure what she would have said).

I can remember in one of our many conversations how she explained to us the importance of children having the good sense of knowing the values of their parent's sacrifice. Can you imagine the amount of discipline and self-sacrifice that it took to meet her parents' every expectation in such a way that she held on to every last word? The thought of disobeying her father drove fear in her that even during the conversation she would break out in a smile and say: "my dad was very strict." Some of the earliest memories of my mother's conversation were pretty basic to the point where she never explained in detail about anything else she had ever done.

My grandmother was strict and forceful. I never met her but I could imagine as a young boy going to the country on summer vacations, it probably wasn't something I would look forward to, so I kind of got the impression of what Charolette's life was like growing up. Mother, who had lived in the community most of her teenage years, was loved by most of the older people who knew her because of the discipline she had shown over the years. She explained that when she was a child, she had never thought of going anywhere else other than staying in the country with her parents. Therefore, Charolette lived her life in a bubble and did not understand being outside of that environment and what it was like to see and enjoy the beauty of this awesome paradise.

I remembered once we were talking about what her life was like in her early days. She sat back for a while as if she were contemplating her answer or figuring out the best way to articulate her early rearing in the rural area of the island. Maybe she thought I was now old enough to understand. Then she started to smile.

"Son, I grew with strict parental monitoring, especially by my father. You see, I was a beautiful little girl growing up in the community with long beautiful hair, so I guess my parents were protective. They wanted me grow up in a certain kind of way. You see, in those days, parents will let you know, you should marry a doctor or a lawyer. Never sure where they got that concept from. So I lived my life trying to emulate them in every possible way. I went to school as was expected, to church, to the fields, wash clothes, tidy the house, sweep the yard, and numerous other things. I wasn't allowed to go out."

Charolette's smile faded as her mind took her back to another place and time. I was quiet as I listened to her voice and I felt like I too had been transported with her.

Young Charolette Erica Elliott sat staring at the pages of the Bible on her lap. It was evening, the tropical sun just setting and giving the hills around a heavenly glow. Her homework was done; everything was ready for the next day.

The Silent Hurt of Charolette Erica Atwell

Outside, the squeals of children playing at dusk came to her ears. Her mind drifted to thoughts of the games they were playing: dandy-shandy, rounders, and perhaps 'one and twenty'. Their voices rang out in the cool evening and Charolette felt a small ache in her chest that she was forbidden from joining them. Her mother, Helen, sat across from her like a guard, humming a song as she sat in her rocking chair, and sewing with her needle and thread at the hem of her husband's pants.

Charolette was often called by her middle name Erica. She was close to her mother; her father was another matter. Philip Elliott was a disciplinarian and so he was very intimidating and forceful. He was never a person who would abuse or punish Charolette in any way that would cause harm to her; but he was a man of few words and stern in his instructions. Erica grew up learning to be independent and self-reliant in her daily duties as a child.

The small village was a quiet place. There wasn't much at that time in the way of entertainment; children had to find ways to amuse themselves. What the adults did for enjoyment was known only to them. There were no parties or special functions except maybe a wedding or two and often a nine-night celebration for a recently deceased. Then, everyone would bring food and stay up all night with the family of the deceased until the funeral.

As the night settled in, so did a quiet over the village. The only sounds Charolette could hear were insects whistling all night and somewhere a donkey braying or a dog barking. The rooster would wait until the early hours of the morning to crow and wake the whole village up to start the day.

The Silent Hurt of Charolette Erica Atwell

The small village watched as Charolette blossomed into a young woman. She went to church with her parents. She read her bible daily and did what she was supposed to do. And she avoided boys like her parents admonished her.

Being intimate with a boy without being married was an abomination in the sight of her parents and the elders of the community. It was seen as a disgrace and an embarrassment to the family and friends. Many a young girl who unfortunately got caught up in or involved in a relationship and eventually got pregnant were ostracized by the community at large.

It was early in her teenage years that one of her dear friends fell victim to the ignorance and sometimes-brutal concept of sex outside of marriage as a reason to be cast out and shown disdain. It was a shock to Charlotte, first, because she had no idea that her friend was engaging in an intimate relationship with a man. The whole community was in an uproar and every young girl found herself under their watchful eyes as if that would prevent anyone else from falling victim.

Seeing the response of the people made Charolette deathly afraid of being in a relationship that would cause an embarrassment to her parents. The family was looked up on in the community as examples of Christian family values, so it would be a total disappointment if that should happen to Charolette.

Charolette was really blooming at seventeen years old and her parents and community felt proud of the upstanding young woman she had become. She walked with a stride to her hips and a straightness to her back that told the world that she meant business. Philip and Helen Elliott worried for their daughter, the pride and joy of their lives, even though they had two other younger children.

Her parents would make sure that whatever she wore to go outside of the house, even to the shop was scrutinized by her mother. Charolette's mother would make sure that whatever she had on was properly secured and tied a certain way. When Charolette came back from the store, the knot would meticulously be inspected for any signs that it had been loosened or tied in a different way. That process carried on for a while without ceasing.

Young Charolette's hurt was silent. She dared not tell her mother that this was demeaning and hurtful. For her to even question such actions would be a sign of insubordination and therefore the consequence could be severe and painful. Her resentment grew daily; but she could not think of rebelling.

Charolette was articulate from a young age and had a good concept of what her life would be like, according to her parents. She had no concept of what she herself aspired to be. She only knew that when the time came a nice young man would come to court her, ask her father for her hand in marriage, and they would get married and live in their own home with their family. There was no thought of Charolette being anything else.

How it began, Charolette could not say. But, after a while her parents' control got to her and a rebellious streak began to develop. Boys were pursuing her. They called out to her as she passed to go to the shop or just about anywhere. They were telling her the things that a beautiful young woman wanted to hear. Charolette started to act and do things she wouldn't normally do to irk her parents, especially her father Philip, who was extremely protective of his only daughter.

Finally, Charolette just went "rogue," experiencing everything that young girls did, even though she knew the consequence would be severe. One night, Charolette snuck into the house through an open window. She had not realized how late it was; she was having such a grand time. Her father stood waiting in the dim light cast by the lamp in the living room. He was silent.

The punishment he meted out to her was so severe she had to stay in the house for many days and could not come outside. Bruises were too visible; swollen skin and marks all over her body were too obvious to be seen in public. Parents, of course, had the right to beat the living crap out of their children if and when they misbehaved. Furthermore, the community at large also had the right to discipline any child of the community when they stepped out of line; and after administering the punishment, parents would be advised of the reason(s) the child was slapped around or spanked. The child was too out of order, was usually the verdict.

Charolette basked in the attention she was getting from the boys. After being caged up and finding a little bit of freedom, she ran wild in trying to experience all the things she had missed. Charolette smiled through swollen lips as she recalled her first sexual encounter, her face lighting up. It had not been what she had expected. Charolette had thought from the conversation she had with her friends who had gone down that road and told her about the experience that it was all fun and good feelings.

And then it happened: Charolette got pregnant the first time she stepped out of the guidelines of her parents' rules and regulations about being celibate and saving herself for her husband. That experience was very traumatic for her. Hiding her pregnant state was not an easy thing; but she managed to keep her secret for a while. But only for a while.

"Erica, you look like you carrying," the woman suggested as she observed Charolette's small bulge about her waist.

It seemed it *was* true that it took a whole village to raise a child. Apparently, some woman from the community had been observing Charolette for some time.

"No, ma'am," Charolette unequivocally denied.

That was when all hell broke loose because it did not end there. The woman took the liberty of going directly Charolette's mother.

"When last you take a good look at Charolette belly? You don't see Charolette look like she is pregnant?"

That assumption did not sit well with her parents. Charolette was summoned to explain what was going on with her. Charolette, once again, denied her condition; she had no intention whatsoever of telling her parents the truth about being pregnant. The deception continued for a while. What Charolette had not thought about was all the changes women go through during the period of pregnancy.

Finally, Charolette began to understand the significance of her parents' instructions about being careful in her actions and the consequences they could bring.

The Silent Hurt of Charolette Erica Atwell

Philip Elliott was in a state of shock and disappointment knowing his one and only daughter whom he had loved and cared for so much would now become one of the statistics: being pregnant without a future. Despite his strict regimen it seemed none of that was relevant in Charolette's being pregnant; it became depressing and emotionally troubling for him.

Charolette decided to explain to her father the circumstances that led to her condition; he refused to even entertain her reason or condone her action.

That kind of rejection drove Charolette further into uncertainty about her future relationship with her father. Helen looked at her daughter with sympathy. It was not that long ago that she had smiled to herself as the girl studiously read her bible; she had given thanks that her beautiful daughter was not like some of the other girls in the village. She could see her high hopes being dashed to pieces, even though she felt some empathy towards her. That kind of brought some well needed solace to Charolette's already fragile emotional unstable mind.

The First Child

Charolette's shame grew each day but the main concern for her parents was how well this boy who had got her pregnant would accept his responsibility in terms of taking care of her or if he even knew he had got her pregnant. Charolette had not anticipated that her actions would have got that far to begin with. But on the Island, there was always the old saying, "Whatever you sow, you shall surely reap; can't sow corn and reap peas." Charlotte had heard it many times but had never paid it much attention. Simply, whatever you have done in this life, whether good or bad, the consequence is always a part of the process.

Unfortunately, Charolette was left with a child that she hadn't prepared for and had no understanding of the responsibilities that came with rearing a child. She recalled the moment she had stood before her parents who were inquiring who the father of her child was.

"How could you, Erica?" was the question when his name was finally revealed. "A boy with no standing?"

As if it would make her disgrace more bearable if he was from an upstanding family. According to her parents, she could have done better than that; the young man wasn't from a family that was well regarded nor did they meet the standards of her parent's expectations. Well, the horse had already gone through the gate so Helen and Philip decided to go and meet with the boy and his parents to discuss their daughter's future.

That first meeting did not go well. Charolette's parents had already made up in their minds that he wasn't good enough for her. It ended worse than she had even imagined; it was more like being in a bad dream and trying to wake up and being unable get out of the nightmare. That even brought on more resentment on her. Philip turned to his daughter:

"How could you have stoop so low? After all your mother and I have done trying to raise you in a decent and proper way, what have we done to deserve this?"

Charolette broke down in tears trying to justify her actions with her parents. The more she tried to explain her actions it only drove her parents to the edge of hostility towards her. During her pregnancy, she was forbidden to have any kind of relationship or contact with the father of her unborn child. Charolette was torn between wanting to see him and not wanting to defy her parents at this crucial time. Defying her parent's instruction could be detrimental with regards to her having a stable home, financial support, and emotional support and stability. She now understood too well the consequences of being disobedient.

After all that had occurred during the initial stage of her pregnancy, it was required of her to have a different outlook on life. Her parents made clear that she had to do everything in her power to win back their trust and respect. Hesitation wasn't an option. Moving forward, she had to adhere to every bit of counseling and criticism with every fiber of her being, although at times she had to bite her tongue not to respond in a disrespectful way. She knew the consequence would be severe in having somewhere to stay. From there in, Charolette was on her best behavior, trying not to evoke the wrath of her parents who already had a strained relationship with her because of the mistake she had made.

Over the months to follow, the tension remained the same. Charolette was able to see her unborn child's father on a few occasions without her parents' consent or knowledge. Her feelings for him became emotionally charged and missing him was making her life more difficult with each passing day. Each time they would meet, the information where to meet and when would be communicated through her best friend; the friend would also be the lookout person in case anyone should see them both together.

The young man's parents tried unsuccessfully to reason with Charolette's parents to at least come to some kind of compromise where the young man could be a part of the child's life. The Elliotts weren't having it. Their daughter had shamed them enough already. They did not need her meeting up with the man who had helped her bring them into disgrace.

One night, Charolette began feeling pains under her belly. She was in labor. She asked her mother to please let the young man know she was going into labor. Helen looked at her in disdain; she wasn't having it in any shape or form. The idea was soundly rejected with strong reprimands and choice words that drove Charolette deeper into depression.

The journey to the nearest hospital was quite a few miles. Transportation was difficult because of the terrain and limited road access. A vehicle in top condition could barely maneuver the rugged road. Philip, her dad got up, lit his torch, and walked about two hundred meters to one of the persons in the community who had a car that could take Charolette to the hospital.

The Silent Hurt of Charolette Erica Atwell

After returning home with this beautiful boy child, the glow in Charolette's face was bright and serene. Even more, the pride and joy in her parents' eyes was priceless after all that had occurred during the whole pregnancy. Helen held onto the child as if there were no tomorrow, cuddling and rocking back and forth, singing these beautiful lullabies to this innocent and precious gift of life. All, it seemed, was forgiven and forgotten with the birth of the precious angelic being.

A week later, the young man and his parents requested to see the child and were rudely reprimanded. The look on the young man's face registered his feelings of hurt, pain and rejection. His parents weren't going to sit around and watch their child go through that kind of traumatic experience. In the heat of the argument, some mean things were said on both sides. Charolette sat there in a daze, contemplating how this unfortunate circumstance could become such a burden to everyone outside the actual parents.

"Who is entitled to make the decisions about our new born child? It is outrageous to see the divisiveness. It pains my most inner being," Charolette murmured to herself, not wanting to upset her parents.

At one point, she tried to get both parents to reach some kind of agreement; that effort was quickly dismissed. Days turned into weeks and weeks turned into months before one beautiful spring morning, while the breeze was blowing from the eastern end of the island, Charolette decided it was about time the father of the child got a chance to see and bond with his child. Before Charolette left the house, her childhood friend was there so the message was sent to for him to meet her at the place where they had their first encounter.

When he arrived and saw her, they both held onto each other with a passion that was warm, and emotional tears were the only language spoken for about ten minutes. Then they realized that baby Jacob was in between them. They sat on a piece of log with the baby in his father's arms holding him tight like a mother bear protecting her cub from a predator. It was a joy to see two young lovers who had this love and passion for each other, separated by differences that had nothing to do with them both. Right there and then they made a promise to each other that no matter what happened they would be there for each other through thick and thin. Both swore to each they would do everything possible to raise baby Jacob to the best of their abilities.

Charolette left the place where long standing memories were first realized. On her way back home, she was beaming with joy. Her demeanor was one of peace and happiness.

Unfortunately, that joy didn't last for long. While they were at their secret spot, one of the older neighbors in the community had seen them. She did not hesitate to inform Charolette's parents of seeing her and the young man. Her dad did not say much; her mother was more upset and fuming mad. Then she made it abundantly clear:

"If that is what you want to do with your life, go ahead. You'll end being a statistic with a whole lot of children and no one to take care of them, because you're a stubborn child."

The Silent Hurt of Charolette Erica Atwell

Charolette assured her parents she wouldn't fall to the difficulties of what they perceived as "worthless" and the mistakes of other young girls in the community was not a reflection of what she would become. After what she had endured, Charolette decided she would do everything in her power to win back the trust of her parents. Although it was a tumultuous relationship, her parents meant the world to her, and the last thing she would want to do was see them hurt or not living up to her fullest potential. The relationship between her and her parents had grown tremendously over a period of time that brought them closer. At some point during this transition period of mother daughter relationship, her mother brought up the topic of the young man.

"I need to know what are your intentions and his. If he's going to be a good father that would provide for you and take care of you and the child, your father and I will give you our blessings?"

When her mother finished, the tears were already flowing. She hugged her tightly and reminded her how much she loved her. Charolette then make the bold move and went to her father who was sitting in his comfort chair on the porch looking over the vast land of every fruit and provision you could think of. Charolette nervously asked in a trembling voice:

"Dad, I can talk with you?"

To her amazement he replied:

"Certainly," with no signs of anger or rage.

Charolette thought for a moment: *is this real or am I dreaming?* From the previous conversations, *this* was a total three hundred and sixty degree turn. She sat close to him and said:

"Dad, let me first apologize to you for getting pregnant without being married. I know deep down in your heart that you had wanted for me to grow in a respectable manner. Unfortunately, I decided to go against your will and the consequence was the birth of a child. I need to assure you I will definitely make you proud of me. "

After she said that, he turned to her in a manner she had never seen before. With a broken spirit and contrite heart he said to her:

"My daughter, you mean the world to me. My only hope for you has always been that you would grow up to accomplish everything that this precious life has to offer. I don't want you to end up suffering in this God-forsaken place where young lives are just wasted away, not because of their choice, but the environment allows that to happen. There is a whole world out there waiting for you with a lot of opportunity. I never want you think this is all that life is about, my child. But have courage to know that what you put out is what you received back. What I am trying to say to you is make every effort not to confine yourself to being average. You are a smart and intelligent young woman."

Charolette was dumbfounded. She could not find the words to respond because, in all the years she had known her dad, he had given her the impression that he was this strong, unemotional human being. He walked with his head held high and was just so stoic and intellectually sound; so hearing him being vulnerable was refreshing. After he finished his pep talk, Charolette turned to him, hugged him, and whispered in his ears:

The Silent Hurt of Charolette Erica Atwell

"I love you more than you'll ever know. My promise to you is that I'll make you proud of me. I will accomplish everything that this life has to offer. Hopefully, you'll be around to enjoy the fruits of your labor."

Tears he was trying to hold back seeped from the corners of his eyes. He had shocked himself at what he had revealed to his daughter, especially knowing how all his life he had portrayed himself as this strong disciplinarian.

That day, the previous strained relationship between Charolette and her parents changed. They decided that Jacob's father would be allowed to come by the house and visit his child. Even though no word was ever spoken to the child's father by Charolette's parents, it was obvious that they had come a long way in showing some kind of acceptance of what they could not change.

The main stipulation was that he would come by at a specific time set by Philip and Helen and would have to leave at a specific time; he wasn't allowed to be there when either or both of them was not at home.

The ground rules were set and needed to be followed. Charolette didn't mind at first. It was part of her agreement with herself and with her parents that she would show them respect and follow their rules at all times. After all, it was this breaking of their rules that had got her into trouble in the first place. On top of that, they had now forgiven her and were showing her so much love and support that it would be just so wrong for her to disobey them or show them any form of disrespect.

Charolette felt lucky. She had her parents' support; not all girls in her position were this fortunate. For most, both their parents and the community had shunned them, leaving them to fend for themselves or move to another part of the island to help keep the family name and pride safe and secure from the disgrace. For this blessing, Charolette was eternally grateful.

Tragedy in the Family

Little Jacob was growing so well. His cheeks were chubby and his little legs sturdy as he tumbled about like a little man. His eyes could melt the hearts of his mother and grandparents with just one look. The community could not be angry with this sweet child because of the circumstances of his birth, although he secretly served the purpose of the other mothers who were raising their own daughters. He was their reminder to any wayward seeking girls of the consequences of children not obeying their parents. He also brought Charolette and her parents closer together. Her relatives and friends eventually came to accept what had happened and Charolette was almost returned to her position of high favor in the family.

Philip Elliot was overwhelmed with joy each time he held Jacob in his arms and bounced him on his knee. As the evening sun was about to set, he would sit on the porch, a faraway look on his face. He wasn't a man of many words, but just looking at his tall stature and beautiful silver hair, his presence was very hard not to notice. Charolette was extremely fond of him and was just smitten by his kindness and loving ways; she decided that when she got married her husband would have to at least possess some of the qualities that she saw in her dad Philip.

Jacob was still a tiny toddler when Charolette's dad started complaining about feeling some unusual pains in his stomach. Charolette was concerned for her dad's health because she had never really seen him sick before. He was a hard-working man who left early in the morning to tend to his livestock and farming, and returned home at the end of the workday, exhausted but with an appetite for the food his wife spread out in front of him on the table. The glow on his face was enough to tell he was a healthy and happy man, despite how hard he worked.

On a few occasions, Charolette would see him writhing in agony and it was obvious on his face that the pain was excruciating. Their conversation seemed to be always the same:

"Dad, would you like a cup of tea?" Charolette asked as she leaned over him, a look of concern on her face.

"I'll be fine. It's just a little gas pain," he would respond.

Charolette's concern grew. She knew full well that this wasn't just any other pain and she encouraged him to see a doctor. But the stubbornness was too great of a challenge.

Helen was even more concerned for his health. They were married long enough for her to know that he would rather suffer in silence than cry out for help. Helen never understood the logic of that concept. Philip Elliott rose early every morning to go and start his day in the fields and looked after his livestock and the farm. He believed that when you start that early, you get a lot more accomplished for the day. He always thought that it was lazy people who lay in bed until sun-up and thought that they were bad elements in the society, because they didn't know the value of work.

Charolette watched her father carefully. She learned so much from him during that period of her life that she sometimes wondered what it would be like not having him around. She tried not to think about that possibility. But, since Jacob's birth, she had begun to see her father in a new light. He was a man of strong principles who provided for his family beyond measure. Nothing was too good for them. She knew if she met someone who wanted to marry her, he would have to be much like her father.

Yes, he had been rough on her and her feelings during the time she was pregnant. Now she understood that it was only his disappointment in her that had made him behave that way toward her. He was kind and loving in his own quiet way.

Charolette and her mother watched over him like a pair of Mother Hens, always making sure that he was alright. They knew what a good man they had in Philip Elliott and that it was absolutely imperative that they showed him the commitment for holding the family together. Charolette's two younger brothers Paul and Joshua could not do much except for the daily chores common to all younger children in the village. However, it was now evident that they would have to take a different approach in assisting with daily chores beyond their years.

Helen sat with her sons and explained in her sweet, calm voice, the importance of taking responsibility to make sure some of things that were being done by their dad were taken care of. The boys were very concerned about what was going on but were afraid to ask too many questions. They could see, despite her efforts, that their mother and older sister were agitated.

When Helen finished talking with her sons, they were themselves left in a state of confusion not knowing the details or circumstance or truly understanding why they would have to take on a more active role in the home. Charolette worked side by side with her mother to get things done that would have been Helen's sole responsibility. It was not easy because little Jacob was becoming a handful. But Charolette hated to see her parents suffer in this way. Despite all their efforts to make things easier, Philip Elliott's health deteriorated into a state of critical care and he could no longer go to his beloved fields or take care of his animals.

One night, while he was laying down, he called his wife to his bedside and hugged her. His once vibrant face was now pale and his cheekbones sunken. Then, he whispered to the woman who had promised to love and cherish him until death does part:

"My love, you are the most wonderful human being God has ever put on this earth. You have been a source of inspiration and a true friend. My undying love for you is more than you can imagine and, if I had to live my life over again, I pray that God would allow you to be a part of it. For the many sacrifices you have made for me and your children. For loving and caring for everyone who comes in your presence is timeless and pure and I love you with even my last breath."

Helen's mood became solemn. She sat there next to his bed with tears in her eyes flowing steadily, holding on to him for dear life, and never speaking a word. Helen just stared at him with this peaceful look on her face as if she had accepted what was to be. The scene before them humbled Charolette, Paul, and Joshua and they stood in silence listening to their father say those amazing words to a woman who had been nothing but a virtuous woman.

When the family finally decided to take Philip Elliott to the hospital the following morning, it was the same neighbor who had taken Charolette to the hospital when it was time for her to give birth.

The Silent Hurt of Charolette Erica Atwell

The gentleman was willing and somewhat in a state of denial because he and Philip had been friends all their lives; so to see him ill in such a manner was painful for him. After returning home from the hospital a few days later, Philip was not showing signs of improving. He became withdrawn and was even questioning himself as to what he had done to deserve this.

He could barely move his body much less do things for himself. That was probably one of the most difficult things for him to accept since he was a man of independence and great pride.

One night Helen prayed and kissed him goodnight as usual. Philip Elliott did not wake up the next morning. Charolette was in her small room with Jacob when she heard a loud scream coming from her parents' room. Charolette grabbed Jacob from off her bed and she and her brothers rushed toward the sounds.

Helen was laying beside her husband, hugging him close and crying.

"Philip, get up," she pleaded. "Oh, no. Please, God, don't take him from me."

That was a moment Charolette would always have in her memories as a painful moment in time, seeing her mother holding on to the man she had loved for so long and the only one she ever knew. Paul and Joshua never said much but the tears were falling down their faces. It was evident by their stares of bewilderment that they probably were thinking, "What are we going to do now that the one person who taught us how to live a rewarding life full of discipline and love is gone?"

Helen finally rose and held all three of her children close. Baby Jacob still slept, unaware of the painful moment when a loved one expires.   Helen wept uncontrollably; then she whispered:

"God never give us more than we can bear. We will move on as a family. We'll find a way to keep this family together."

Charolette never really cried while all of this was happening; but, after the initial period of mourning, she found herself locked in her room crying with abandon. Her pain and feelings of hopelessness were too much for her to bear.

The old saying "time heals all wounds" seemed to be true as the family carried on after the death of Philip Elliott. They each fell back into their routine of carrying out daily chores; only now, their work was doubled without the man of the house to carry his lion's share.

Helen Rowe Elliott grew quiet. She missed her husband. She would sit on the porch in the evenings looking as if she was   waiting   just   to   see   him   walking up that little hill leading to the house with that big smile on his face. Charolette and her brothers took a more active role in the daily cleaning of the house and the preparation of the evening meals.

They could see their mother's pain as she tried to function alone, something she was not used to doing. They allowed her to just sit back and meditate on whatever it was. There were times she would just give this cheeky little smile to them as if she was acknowledging the fruits of her labor. Jacob was turning into a sweet little boy and became

The Silent Hurt of Charolette Erica Atwell

Helen's reason for wanting to live past a certain age; she was determined to see him grow up.

After Charolette's father died, she didn't have much time for Jacob's father. They had somehow grown apart. One of the things that was troubling was, he wasn't showing interest in how Charolette was feeling during the passing of her father. He made some statement about her father's death that was extremely offensive. That only drove a wedge between them. It became clear that his intentions weren't as good as she had initially thought, so she decided to focus on raising her child and be there for her mother no matter what.

The arguments between them were childish. He bickered over the slightest thing and then got very angry; once he even tried to get physical with her. Charolette was shocked and disappointed to see that the person she loved would want to hurt her.

As Jacob grew, he became more attached to his grandmother. She would take him everywhere with her. To see this happy child which had been born out of love was just the ultimate gift anyone could ever ask for. But, with the death of the main breadwinner, life became difficult financially, as well as emotionally for the family. The financial aspect was much more critical because there were days when they couldn't find anything that they used to enjoy when Philip was alive.

Helen took on the responsibility of making sure the family never went to bed hungry. She started to look for work, which really was nonexistent in that small community. There was hardly anyone who had more than another did. The Elliotts had come a long way down from the comfort in which Philip had kept them. Not that it had been easy; but at least they never wanted for the necessities and the family always kept its dignity.

Early one morning, Helen got up from her bed, dressed, and whispered in Charlotte's ears that she was going out and would be back before dinnertime.

"Be careful," Charolette whispered back in her ear.

"I love you, my child," Helen promised.

That day, Charolette was left to take care of her siblings, something she had never done before. It was overwhelming, especially with trying to take care of Jacob too. She had mostly watched her mother take the lead in performing the daily duties for her family and had learned a few things over the years that she could apply. But she had never been left solely responsible for all the duties of the home.

During the whole day, Charolette took full charge of the responsibility of keeping the house clean. Jacob was fed and her brothers were properly dressed and had breakfast before they left for school. When she had completed all the chores about the middle of the day, she was exhausted.

Worn out, she sat on a piece of log in the kitchen. It came to her clearly: Helen had been doing this kind of work for a mighty long time but she had never heard her complain one day about the difficulties. In that moment, Charolette had a new appreciation for her commitment to her family.

Jacob was a good boy that day. He was constantly, asking for "nana". He had become so attached to his grandmother so not seeing her was unusual for him. Charolette gave him a bath and told him that grandma would be back soon.

The Silent Hurt of Charolette Erica Atwell

That day, Jacob's father showed up. She was not sure if he knew her mother was away and that Charolette was home by herself.

"What you are doing here?" Charolette asked as he approached.

Because of their previous encounter, Charolette was a little apprehensive being with him alone, although a part of her was glad he was there and she was glad for the company. They sat and talked about what had happened with his outburst of anger. He was very apologetic and promised he would never do anything stupid like that again. Right there and then the emotions and longing for him came back like a raging flood inside Charolette.

She had wanted him for a long time; it was like a drought for her not having any sexual contact with him since the incident. He reached over and kissed her lips and she melted with passion, wanting that feeling she had felt when they first met. Charolette was in a state of weakness. It was not like she was an unwilling participant. She was just in the moment during that passionate kiss. Next thing she knew, his hands were all over her body. When he touched her vagina, she was already in a place of excitement.

"I miss you so much," he murmured.

Charolette was just groaning and twitching her slender frame in his arms.

They made love that day; it was a beautiful experience since, for the first time, they weren't concerned about who was there or trying to hide. It was in the privacy of her parents' home. After they had finished, they sat there in each other arms, loving what they had just experienced.

The Silent Hurt of Charolette Erica Atwell

Then, they heard that little voice calling "Mommy!" Jacob had woken up.

They dressed hurriedly. Charolette went and picked up the baby and hugged him. Then she took him back to his father. Baby Jacob was kind of resisting his father because he hadn't been a part of his life that much due to the restrictions placed on her by her parents. Gently, Charolette coaxed the baby and reminded him that this was his dad. When Jacob finally reached over into his father's arms, the young man's face lit up like a bright bulb shining in a dark, lonely, and desolate place. He fed him; it was pure joy seeing the meticulous approach he took holding his child, making sure he did everything right. Charolette was happy to see that he was able to show his child the care for even that moment. It was the right thing to do.

As the day was coming to an end Charolette reminded him he had to leave now because her mother would be home at any time and would be upset coming home and seeing them alone together. She was very concerned for that not to happen because she had worked so hard to build the trust between herself and her parents; she could not afford to jeopardize the whole thing. Furthermore, for what her mother was going through with the death of her husband it would be devastating in many ways. So Charolette was deliberate in her actions; he was kind of resisting, but she knew that the best course of action would be for him to leave.

About an hour after he left, Charolette's brothers returned from school. Not seeing their mother, they asked, "where is mommy?" Charolette reminded them to go and take off their clothes and start their homework. Having the

The Silent Hurt of Charolette Erica Atwell

opportunity to be that authoritative for just that one moment felt real good to her.

Helen returned just before nightfall with a pleasant look on her face. Charolette was hoping something good had happened.

"You promise never to leave nor forsake us, so I depend on you, oh Lord, to provide for this family, because my hope is in you," Helen said in her still but sweet, beautiful voice. "Make me a cup of tea, Erica."

"Yes, ma'am," Charolette responded with a sense of pride and delight that was the first time she had ever asked her to do anything like that.

Helen never spoke of what her trip was like. Deep down in her heart, Charolette had the notion she had gone in search of a job. After she rested for a while, Helen called Charolette.

"Dear, today I went and found a job. It's not much, but it will be able to us sustain through this difficult transition period."

Helen had found a job taking care of two children in one of the most affluent neighborhoods about seven miles from where they were living. Beyond that, she did not say much more.

"It's not much," she further explained, "but gives us a sense of dignity not to get in a place of being poverty stricken individuals."

Helen was adamant not to watch her family fall apart with regards to not being able to feed them; so whatever was required of her to see her children live a meaningful life she was willing to take as a job.

The Silent Hurt of Charolette Erica Atwell

Some evenings she would come home tired in such a manner she could not even move her hands or legs. Apparently, she did a lot cleaning and standing each day. Many evenings Charolette was too distraught to even ask her how was her day; by the look on her face, it was obvious. There and then, Charolette made the decision that she would never end up like her mother who had depended on her husband for financial support. When he died, he never left much, only the lands that he owned which had been handed down to him by his parents. But what good is having land when there was no one to work it or money to pay someone to do so?

As Charolette watched her mother rise early in the morning and return home late evening, her determination became more and more a priority to do all that was required of her. One evening after Helen returned home, she lay down for a moment and was just twisting and turning as if she was trying to find a comfortable side of her frail body to get a perfect rest. From then Charolette began to pay more attention to her mother; she got the feeling that she was coming to a point in her life where it was more difficult to do some of the things she used to do in the past.

Charolette knew the responsibility was great. She was willing and able to take on the challenges of assisting Helen in any way she could.

Helen was becoming increasingly isolated from her children. Most of the days she would stay locked in her room, singing and humming some of the most inspirational hymns you'll ever hear. Many nights she would be in her room crying, asking God why he had to take the love of her life so soon. She had loved Philip with

The Silent Hurt of Charolette Erica Atwell

every fiber of her being and never really got over losing him. Then one night, Charolette overheard Helen whispering in the darkness that she was ready to go and spend eternity with her husband. Charolette broke down in tears knowing there wasn't much she could do or say.

The Elliotts were a family of secrets. It was instilled in them from early age that "whatsoever goes on in this house will remain in this house. People outside of the immediate family don't need to know the trials and hardships we are facing." So Charolette and her brothers grew up with the notion that they did not seek outside help, whatever the situation might be. Rather they would try and fix or resolve the issue amongst ourselves.

Charolette watched her mother fall into deep depression, slowly without the proper help or diagnosis to help fight the pain of losing her husband. During those days people never really had the basic understanding of what depression was and how it could affect one's ability to function just by doing the simplest thing. When Charolette and her brothers would go to the store or the fields, the neighbors would ask, "how is your mother doing?" They would reply, "she is doing fine," because that's the way they were taught to respond. It was more important to keep their mother isolated and secluded from the nosy neighbors. Like every other small community, the neighbors liked to talk and make assumptions about one's health when they found out someone was sick.

One lonely night, Helen went to bed and never woke up the next morning; she died a lonely and painful death. It seemed she had given up on living for quite some time. She had held on to her husband's passing with such conviction and commitment it became overwhelming and sometimes sad.

After Helen passed, Charolette was in a state of shock for quite a while not knowing what next to do. There she was, left with a young son who was growing into such a beautiful child, and two younger brothers who still needed a mother's attention. She knew she had to be strong for Jacob and her brothers because they also became motherless and fatherless. They basically had become orphans at that stage in their lives. Seeing the strength of her parents in their earlier stages of lives when they were healthy, Charolette learned a great deal about becoming self-sufficient. Now, it was time for her to put into practice what she had learned.

The Second Pregnancy

When it was all said and done, Charolette was on her own now, contemplating her next move in a cynical way. She wasn't too optimistic about the future, or the prospect of achieving anything that would be substantial to her future. Just about that time, Jacob's father had come back into her life. He was a source of strength at a time when she needed it the most. He had started to stay by the house with her brothers and they became much closer and had a better relationship than previous years. Her parents weren't there anymore to obstruct or disapprove of him.

They started off pretty good; he was very helpful and attentive in the beginning of renewing their relationship to the point where he was living with her. As time moved forward, it was a wonderful experience. Then reality quickly sunk in. He wasn't working so life had become a little more burdensome in terms of not having the basic things to provide for her and their son. A few times, they argued over the prospect of him doing something other than what he was doing, like running errands for people in the community. She knew at some point that wouldn't be enough to sustain their responsibilities.

Then the arguments became more intense and more frequent. They were raising their voices using all kinds of derogatory remarks or insinuating some serious accusation. On one occasion, one of her brothers got into an argument with him and explicitly let him know he could not continue treating Charolette this way. Her brother was standing up for her; it felt real good and gave her a feeling of being protected. There were times

Charolette thought that the confrontation would escalate to physical violence; that was how serious it became.

They went through the daily motions of just being there together. For Charolette, the death of her parents and having the responsibility of a young child and caring for the home and her brothers was somewhat overwhelming.

However, being in a sexually active relationship with Jacob's father placed her at risk for getting pregnant again. They had already proven that they were fertile together. Charolette was not using any form of contraceptive and she was just hoping that she wouldn't get pregnant. They did practice safe sex with him pulling out at the moment he was about to climax. For a while, that worked. But then, Charolette's worst fear became a reality.

She missed her period for two months and was in state of shock and disbelief, asking herself how could she let this happen again? She was absolutely sure about not wanting to be pregnant while being in such an uncertain place of emotional distress and not having the means or the help of her parents.

By the fourth month, Charolette decided to go to the midwife who resided about two miles from where she was living to confirm if she was really pregnant. Charolette was in total denial, crossing her fingers as if that would stop her from being pregnant.

The midwife was the same one who had delivered Jacob. She was a strong disciplinarian and stern in her conversation with young adults. The problem was that she was a close family friend and she had given a long pep talk about being pregnant out of wedlock and how much it hurt Charolette's parents seeing her pregnant before getting married. Charolette built up the courage to go to her since there was no alternative. She was the only midwife for miles around.

When Charolette arrived, the midwife was happy to see her.

"How are you managing with all that has happened in such a short space of time?" the woman asked.

Charolette began to cry and explained in between her tears how difficult it was just going through the day without her parents there to help her, and how much she missed them both.

"How is the baby?" the woman asked in her stern voice. "Well," Charolette responded, "he is no baby no more. He is growing to be such sweet child. I just love and adore him."

Charolette's eyes were glowing as she spoke about Jacob. She could not find the courage to tell the midwife why she was really there. So, the chit chat continued about life and what Charolette intended to do with her life. She had been an 'A' student in school and most of the community knew. In this close-knit community, all the parents shared their children's progress in school with each other.

Then the dreaded question raised its ugly head.

"So Charolette, what do I owe this visit for today?"

Still in a state of denial, Charolette replied:

"Nothing. I was just passing and decided to stop by and see how you was doing. "

The midwife quickly turned and looked at Charolette. Her expression was one of disgust and Charolette could feel the all too familiar feeling of rejection. Once again, she had let down her family and the whole community.

"Are you pregnant again?" the midwife demanded.

"I don't know," Charolette stuttered.

"When last you saw your period?"

"About three to four months ago. "

"Oh my Lord, what is wrong with you? Do you how much it hurt your parents when you got pregnant the first time? It broke their heart because they had such high hopes for you. They had struggled to even accept you being pregnant because the community was talking about them in such negative way, about you being pregnant. Your family was held in such a high regards so you being pregnant out of wedlock was a total embarrassment to them."

Charolette went into a state of total dejection, feeling useless and hurt. A part of her started to feel that she was somehow responsible for her parents' death.

"There is no doubt in my mind you're pregnant," the midwife insisted.

Charolette's whole world came crashing down right there and then. Even in that difficult time the midwife was able to give her some words of comfort and wisdom, assuring Charolette that everything was going to be okay. Charolette felt a little bit of relief knowing that there was someone standing on her side. At least someone had some hope for her that she would succeed.

On her way home, there was a lot going through Charolette's mind; it was just running away with thoughts

The Silent Hurt of Charolette Erica Atwell

of 'what's next'. She walked slowly, trying to figure out where to go from there. It was a long walk home.

On arriving home, the look on her face was quite obvious. "What's wrong, mommy," little Jacob asked, a look of concern on his small face.

"Nothing," she responded, "just a little tired from being on the street walking that long journey home. I'll get dinner ready for you to eat and give you a bath. Then I'll come sit and talk with you."

Jacob nodded and ran off to play again.

Charolette was still in a state of shock as she made dinner. She could not accept the fact that she was pregnant again, with no plan of raising a family on her own. The tears were just flowing freely. She could not control the emotions that she was going through. Then suddenly, she made this weird sound in a loud voice. Everyone came running in that little kitchen on the side of the house, asking what was wrong. Charolette was just trembling and shaking; but she assured them that she would be fine.

"What did you do today?" asked the father of her unborn child when he came home.

She did not respond. She just wasn't in the mood to even entertain that conversation at that moment because on many of occasion she had told him that what they were doing was risky and he had assured her it was okay. She wasn't pointing the finger or putting all the blame on him because she had been a willing participant in the whole process.

Finally she found the strength to tell him.

The Silent Hurt of Charolette Erica Atwell

"I went to the midwife today and I am pregnant. I don't think I am ready for a next child. The burden is far too great for me right at this moment. Therefore, I am contemplating an abortion. I don't know how I am going to manage. I can barely manage what we currently have in terms of taking care of ourselves."

"Oh, God!"

He didn't take it too well. He called Charolette all kinds of names, asking how she could be so insensitive in wanting to take an innocent child's life. So then, she asked him:

"Are you ready for a next child? What are your plans to provide for the basic needs for three of us?"

He stood mumbling a whole lot of stuff that she couldn't understand. Charolette's main concern was to make sure moving forward everything would be structured in a way that would be conducive to rearing of their children in a stable home. The conversation got out of control. She was seeing a side of him that she had not seen before was troubling. She tried to tell him to look at it from all angles. She reminded him that in the community they were living in, there were no jobs.

The prospect of getting a real job was dim as the night in that part of the Island. Charolette wasn't trying to be hard or mean spirited but it was absolutely imperative that they made preparations for their expanding family. He was still on the topic of abortion and why would she want to take that route while there were many other options.

"Well, if you see it that way, what is your solution?"

He got real cranky and went on to say that she always felt that she was better than him and that he knew she wanted to leave him a long time ago. Charolette made it clear that it was never her intention to leave him; the fact of the matter was that they were now at a different place in life with greater responsibilities to deal with.

Finally, she got him to sit down and have a meaningful conversation about what they were going to do moving forward to benefit them both and their family. One thing was abundantly clear; Charolette wasn't going to sit around depending on him to take care of her and the children. From that summer evening, Charolette's whole concept of what it meant to achieve the best possible outcome in any situation was to do the things that will allow you to grow and become independent so she was sure of her intentions.

During the pregnancy, they kind of grew apart. It was a reoccurrence of what had happened during the first pregnancy. This time was a little different though because it wasn't her parents in the middle of it; he was just being a total jackass about it. Many a night Charolette was alone in pain and needed his assistance. He was nowhere to be found; nor did he have the decency to stop by and see how she was doing or if she needed anything.

Charolette began feeling a rejection for him; his actions were unbecoming and he was noticeably absent from his responsibilities. One evening, he stopped by after having been absent for a period of time. Charolette was already in a bad mood and wasn't going to entertain his in and out behavior, showing up when he wanted to as if she was irrelevant and had no concept of what it meant to be committed.

She explained to him that she was at the point of giving up on the relationship because of his total disregard for her and his children. Their relationship never returned to the previous years when they had first started; it was downhill after she became pregnant with the second child. He had started to have extra relationships, cheating, and carrying on as if she was insignificant to him. She wasn't going to fall out of character to please him or even give him the satisfaction to feel important. Anyhow, she was determined to move on with her life and became more committed to raising both kids in the best possible way she could. Charolette had a great upbringing her parents who were strong disciplinarians but also loving and kind, so she had a good idea of what it took to nurture and care for children.

One Saturday evening, Charolette sat on the same porch that she'd seen her parents sit on so many times looking at the gleaming sun going down, just talking and sharing with each other these beautiful stories of their upbringing and the struggles of life in general and what they wanted for their children. She was reflecting on the goodness of her parents and how much she missed them when she saw a young woman coming up the hill. The house was built in a way you could actually see the end of the road. Charolette didn't recognize the woman but she wasn't concerned because it was customary for people to just stop by. People were mostly honest and open and violence toward another was almost unheard of. People might get into a quarrel about a stray animal that was eating someone's provision ground or some such small disagreement. The next day they would be neighbors and friends again.

The Silent Hurt of Charolette Erica Atwell

As the young woman got closer, Charolette recognized her as a class mate from Primary school. She called out to her.

"How are you? What are you doing up this way? I haven't seen you in a long time?"

"I'm fine," she responded. "I'm here to see you."

Being naïve, Charolette never thought much about the visit; she was just so glad to see someone to talk to. The women sat on the porch and started to talk about life in general and about each other's lives.

"Charolette, I have to tell you something," the woman said in all seriousness after they had laughed about the old days. "I never meant to hurt you."

Charolette's face dropped as if she knew what was coming. "I am pregnant," she explained.

She was pregnant for Charolette's children's father. Charolette felt her knees buckle even though she was sitting down. Being the optimist she was, a part of her was thinking that the girl was not being truthful; she just lying knowing Charolette was his children's mother.

"How long has this been going on?" Charolette questioned softly.

"Quite a while," she explained.

She could not keep their relationship a secret any longer because she wanted to be with him. Charolette turned to her as if she wasn't hurting inside.

"Well, what can I say? Congratulations to you, and if that's what both of you want that's fine. I wish you all the best."

The girl stared at Charolette in confusion. This was certainly not what she had expected to hear coming up that

The Silent Hurt of Charolette Erica Atwell

hill and revealing her affair with Charolette's lover. After she left, the tears flowed freely down Charolette's face. She could hear the voice of her parents warning her about the relationship. If only she had just listened to her parents she wouldn't be in this predicament. Philip Elliott especially had been skeptical; now he had proved everything her father had warned her about was right. She could feel his spirit saying, "I told you so." She cringed, imagining how much it would have torn him apart if he were alive to see his misgivings about the young man prove true.

Charolette was extremely glad she never showed any sign of breaking down in front of him. Her pride wouldn't allow her to do so. She was hurt and bitter for a long time. After all that she had gone through just to be with him, defying her parents and this was the thanks she got. He hurt her to the core of her being.

After that encounter, Charolette had a new outlook on life: whatever she needed to do, she had to learn not to wait on anyone or anything to fulfill her destiny. She had to take the initiative to go out and do whatever it took to provide for herself and her children. She didn't see him for some time. She eventually got used to not having him around; furthermore, her love for him had diminished drastically. She had never really thought about what she would do if she should lose him. Now, she started to re-focus on the kids and their future. It was one of the most difficult times of Charolette's life knowing the man who was the father of her children was not going to marry her. Instead, he had demeaned her and made her feel guilty, not to mention his relationship with another woman.

After the relationship ended, there was some animosity on both sides. Charolette was in a state of hurt and pain,

The Silent Hurt of Charolette Erica Atwell

knowing she had given her love and self to someone she had thought would be there for her. She had defied her parents for him and had brought shame on their name.

One day, he stopped by the house to visit his children. They hadn't seen him in such a long time. Charolette was skeptical of the visit so she didn't pay him much attention. She had been taught from an early age to never try to keep children away from their father because at some point that child will grow and decide for himself or herself.

First and foremost, he came empty handed despite knowing the struggles she was going through at that time. Charolette never intended to ask for anything because she could guarantee that would come with a price and she wasn't willing to sacrifice her dignity for him again. Her pride would not allow her to, so she grind her teeth and told herself, "Charolette, you're not going to stoop down to a level of desperation and compromise your self- esteem in any shape or form," even though a part of her was saying, "Swallow your pride and ask."

They sat for a little while and the conversation about his cheating ways came up. He had some of the most pathetic excuses for his behavior. Never, at any time did he want to take responsibility for his actions. It almost drove her insane listening to his garbage. After sometime, the conversation became a little more civilized. Charolette realized it wasn't about her or him; the welfare of the children was way more significant. They were able talk well through the evening until it was time for him to go home. Then the *how much I miss you* raised its ugly head. Charolette listened for a while. Then, she began to feel frustrated and angry and asked him to leave and never come back. Watching him walk away, Charolette felt a

The Silent Hurt of Charolette Erica Atwell

burden ease off her shoulder. She knew this was their good bye, but she had had enough.

Sitting in the chair that her parents had sat on for many years watching the evening sun going down, Charolette thought to herself, "My parents must be very proud of me for what I just did." Their constant reminders about standing up for what you believe in never went in vain. Charolette looked around her. There was no one to give her a word of comfort or just a gentle reminder, to say, "It's going to be alright." She was all alone in the world.

A part of her was struggling with the notion that she was now left alone with no source of income, no parental guidance, and no support for the children, and most of all being outright scared of the unknown. Suddenly, it seemed she was hearing her mother's beautiful soft voice whispering in her ear, "If you live long enough to experience the valleys where all seems like its lost, or experience the abundance of life where everything you will need is automatically given to you, then you're in a world by yourself and not thinking logically."

"Thank you, mother," she whispered back.

Charolette realized that she needed that reality check to remind her that life was full of disappointments. From that day forward, Charolette had a new outlook on life. Things that she used to take personal or get easily upset over she was learning to be more pro-active in discerning what the future held. Things might have seemed dim at that time, but there was a sense of pride and jubilation knowing that all was not lost. That period or phase of her life undoubtedly transformed Charolette's critical thinking skills to a new level of responsibility. The process wasn't

The Silent Hurt of Charolette Erica Atwell

easy, but it was a commitment in terms of redirecting her focus and energy on a more pressing issue, that is, the children she needed to feed, clothe, and worry about what their future held.

As Charolette sat there wondering whether she had done the right thing or not in banishing her children's father from her life, she heard a voice as if from afar shouting her name. She didn't recognize the person at first but as the woman came closer she realized it was one of her aunts who was just too self-righteous and a strong disciplinarian.

As a child growing up, her aunt had always been there with Charolette's mother, talking and just laughing out in such loud manner. Sometimes, Charolette wondered what could they be talking about that could have brought laughter and giggles? She had stopped by just to see how Charolette was doing and to see if she needed any help. They were a close-knit family who, despite their differences, always believed in looking out for each other so it was no surprise when she showed up.

She sat in the same spot she would always sit in when both she and Helen were just having conversation about everything that was going on within the community at that time. Charolette was ecstatic to see her because after her mother had died, her aunt never really came around as often as she used to. Charolette knew she had taken her sister's death to heart and she was also struggling with some emotional issues. She was dealing with many unanswered questions about her sister's passing and why.

Charolette and her aunt were able to sit there and talk. At one point, Charolette found herself engaged in the type of conversation usually reserved for adults. That is when she realized, "Oh my, I am becoming like mother." That experience was kind of surreal and somewhat unnatural. In essence, she was just like her mother whether she liked it or not. The conversation led from one thing or another. Charolette knew that her aunt was about to ask her questions regarding the children's father; she had got a sense from early on out that would be a topic up for discussion so she was somewhat prepared.

"So how is the children?" her aunt inquired. "And how is the good for nothing father? When last you spoke to him and what is he doing with his life?"

Charolette was aware how abrupt her aunt could be. She was known as someone who didn't mince her words. Only she would have the audacity to even say that without a blink on her face. It kind of caught Charolette off guard, anyway. She was in a state of shock and also utter disbelief about her approach.

"I am not sure what the status on him is because he was here earlier today and I told him I didn't want anything to do with him."

Her aunt paused for a while as if she had heard some terrible news; she had this look of gloom and disappointment on her face. Charolette was feeling even more guilty thinking to herself, "I am in a real bad situation." She, felt as if London Bridge had come tumbling down.

"Don't worry," she gently whispered, just like Helen would have.

There was this eerie feeling like she was hearing her mother's voice. Her aunt reassured her that everything was going to be all right. She just needed to take the initiative to take control of her life and take the necessary steps to improve herself. Those words were comforting and poignant; at least she knew she had someone who really cared for me.

Although she was in that place of throwing her own pity party with no invitees, the assurance from her aunt was priceless. Charolette was able to open freely talking about the things that she was currently struggling with. It was refreshing and somewhat a justification of all her pessimistic thoughts.

From that day forward, Charolette was energized to accelerate her intentions of being a better person and pursuing her goals. The objective was to lay the foundation of being first and foremost independent. She recalled her mother's own push to survive after her husband died.

The following morning, Charolette rose early and thought about what her day would be like and the things she needed to do to realize a new way of life. A big part of her knew she did not want to be just a housewife who stayed home and took care of the kids or even become so entrenched in the norm of *women work is in the kitchen*; she had a vision of her life/future in a more productive way, making meaningful contribution. She went through the thought process that morning and started to contemplate all the options available to her. There wasn't much that her community had to offer in the way of work.

Jobs were scarce. It was more of a farming community than anything else. The family lands had long since gone to bush with no one to work them. Those who had jobs traveled far and long to be at their jobs. Charolette had fallen into a place of complacency and did not have the tools necessary to expand her scope of self-reliance until that day when her aunt showed up at the house.

Charolette had never really been close to the people in the community other than the ones who stopped by the house or when she accompanied her mother to the store for food shopping and they would stop to exchange pleasantries. Ironically, Charolette's parents were held in high esteem in the community.

On her way as she walked out, Charolette met an elderly woman who politely said:

"Hi, Charolette, how are you and the children? My prayers always with you. Your mother was a great human being. She has helped so many of us in our time of need that you can't even imagine. May God rest her soul."

Post Mistress

That same day while Charolette was on her way to get a few things from the store for dinner, an older gentleman saw her on the street as she approached the store. He was just staring at her, making her feel uncomfortable. Then in a coarse voice, he said:

"You are beautiful girl. When your mother was about your age that is how she looked."

"Thank you," Charolette responded without stopping.

Charolette had too much going on at the moment to entertain small talk. She had been raised a sheltered child who never got out much; even as an adult, she was still a little timid of people and shied away from confrontation. On reaching the store, Charolette was greeted by the shopkeeper.

"Good morning, Charolette."

"Good morning, sir. How are you?" she responded.

She knew him well from all the years of being sent to the store or accompanying her mother. He was a well-respected gentleman in the community and just about everyone went to him in their time of need.

"How is the kids?" he asked.

"They are doing great, Charolette responded.

"So, what brought you out?"

At that moment, Charolette felt like she must have been living under a cave. That's when she realized, "My God, I am living in a zone all by myself where it is just me, myself and I."

The Silent Hurt of Charolette Erica Atwell

The shopkeeper's wife had been the Post Mistress for the community as far back as Charolette could remember. The woman had been good friends with Helen Elliott and they would chat for long periods whenever Charolette and her mother would go to get the mail from the small space used beside the store for the Post Office. After Charolette purchased the few things she had come to get, she politely said to him:

"Please say hello to your wife for me."

"She is not doing too well," he responded. "She went to the doctor yesterday and the diagnosis is not all that great." Hearing that broke Charolette's heart. She recalled how gentle the woman was as she and Helen talked. Her demeanor was one of pure joy and delight.

The store was empty at that time of the day, so the shopkeeper graciously offered Charolette some extra items to take home. She was grateful for the gesture.

"Don't stay and don't have anything to eat while you have an option here," he counseled. "Your parents were great people who have seen my wife and I through some rough times. So I am forever indebted to them. It would be a dis- service to you and your children not to offer assistance when I can."

Charolette's eyes were filled with tears hearing the great things that were being said about her parents in that short space of time since she had left the house. It was somewhat overwhelming.

"Furthermore, I don't think my wife will be able to continue running the Post Office because of her health," he continued. "At some point I will have to look for someone to assist her with the daily operations. It's not much, but

The Silent Hurt of Charolette Erica Atwell

people are expecting their mail and telegrams in a timely manner. Well, anyway I have to leave now but hopefully I will speak to you again. Remember what I said: don't stay down there and don't have nothing to eat and don't come and let me know."

Charolette took the two bags she had received from the store and started walking down the hill towards the house. Her thoughts were running away with her. *Can this be real, or it just co-incidence or even people just trying to be nice because they knew of the death of both my parents?* She wasn't sure what to think but in the back of her mind she got the sense it was sincere and genuine. She had become the direct beneficiary of all their good deeds and it was a wonderful feeling.

On reaching home, Charolette packed away the contents of the bags but there was one thing that kept replaying over and over in her mind: the thought of being the Post Mistress. Could this be a way for her to have a foundation in providing for herself and her brothers? Right there and then she made up her mind. The following morning she was going back to the store to let the shopkeeper know that if the opportunity presented itself she would gladly accept the challenge of being the Post Mistress for the Post Office in the community.

That night, Charolette went to bed with a whole lot on her mind. She thought of the sacrifice and selflessness of her parents to become such a blessing to those whom they had come in contact with. She was just in awe of the mere fact that people were so honored to have known them. She knew deep down that she had a lot to live up to in terms of standards, not so much regulations, but to be honest and forthcoming.

The Silent Hurt of Charolette Erica Atwell

She finally built up the courage the next day to go back to the store and spoke with the shopkeeper. As she entered, for some reason he knew that she was going to ask him about covering the Post Office until his wife was healed.

"So I see you came back," he greeted.

"Yes I did. May I ask you a question?"

"Certainly, "he replied.

"I know I don't have any experience in terms of running a post office, but I am willing to learn to the best of my abilities, if you give me the opportunity,"

The shopkeeper stood there with this weird look on his face for about two minutes as if he was contemplating what he should do. Then he said:

"Charolette, yesterday when I had mentioned it to you, I was hoping you would have ask me to help with running the Post Office. I would be delighted to give you the opportunity to work alongside my wife. I had made a promise to your parents a long time ago that if anything should happen to either of them while I am still living, I would make sure that you don't want for anything. I know you're a smart girl and you have a lot of potential. The pay isn't much but I think you're an honest and well-mannered young lady so you can start next week."

Charolette was overwhelmed with gratitude and joy knowing that even though her parents had died, she became an inheritor of their faithfulness to serve.

So, she started to work at the Post Office. It wasn't much but in terms of staying home without any form of income this was a better option in providing for her basic needs. As time passed, Charolette became increasingly more

The Silent Hurt of Charolette Erica Atwell

intrigued by what she was doing providing service for people who were in need. She found that many of the people who came to the Post Office couldn't read or comprehend a lot of the stuff they were doing or want to do. Then it hit her like a ton of bricks. What her mother and friends used to talk about helping people without looking back for anything in return was a part of their ultimate duties that they took pride in.

Charolette was just amazed at how everything was just coming full circle. She even started to reminisce on things that her mother would say to some of the people she would meet. There was one specific lady whose children had left the rural part of the Island and moved to the city. At least once per week she would stop by the Elliott house and would be in this conversation while Helen wrote. Charolette had never paid much attention then, but now she understood. Now she was in a position where she could emulate her mother's generosity and compassion towards people with no kind of stereotyping or turning up her nose at other people. It was not like she was any richer or more productive than everybody else. But circumstances had come in the way of challenges for the folks of that community. She was now in a place where a lot of things that she would see or hear became strictly confidential so she was held to a standard and stringent principles.

Charolette grew up going to a school which was about two miles to and from where her family lived. She had done well in school and had been told by others that she would turn out to be something great, and to follow her educational path with vigor and commitment. That didn't materialize as she and her parents had expected because of other things which had got in the way. Who was to blame did not matter, but it had stopped Charolette in her tracks and she had veered from the path that was her destiny.

She had wanted so badly to go on to a higher level of education that would be of great benefit to her. She held herself accountable for the bumps, bruises, and missteps she had taken along the journey of life. Now she was getting a chance to change her life. It might not be the way she and her parents had dreamed it, but it certainly was a step in the right direction.

She grew to love being a Post Mistress; it came with some dignity, knowing people were depending on her to take care of their needs. The shopkeeper's wife's health took a turn for the worse so Charolette was left with the responsibility of running the office on a daily basis. The challenge was enormous and required a lot of commitment. But she really had nothing to complain about. Prior to being at the Post Office she was home, unemployed and contemplating all of her options; so in essence, this was a blessing.

At any time during the day, multiple people would stop by to do their mail and other transactions provided by the post office. The level of education received at that time was the basic; unless you were living within the city limit and had the resources to attend a more advanced program in educational studies, it was going to be extremely hard.

Charolette did not realize this job would have required so much from her; just assisting people in general who were struggling to understand the basic sentence structure, she was just amazed. So she started thinking long and hard. That was the first time she really understood the

The Silent Hurt of Charolette Erica Atwell

significance of working in that post office and it had nothing to do with her; it was a much bigger purpose than she thought.

From then she approached everything with a sense of gratitude. A part of her knew she was standing on the shoulders of great people who had laid the foundation of looking out for each other. All the years she had seen her mother give without ceasing, or even gave from the little she had, was quite an example. Charolette's task was to be a person who showed empathy to each and every one at all times.

Charolette recalled in her younger days when her mother would insist when you give, you do so with the intention of not looking back for anything in return, because you never know when you are entertaining strangers that person might be the one who is able to assist on your path in life. Be mindful of how you treat people; you treat people the way you wanted to be treated. Now here she was, practicing everything that had been taught to her as a child. She found herself applying every single thing that her mother had ever done in helping people; a lesson learned.

Some elderly folks who were living alone found solace in just coming to the post office to talk; apparently there was no one else to talk to or share whatever they were going through. Some of their children had already left the community to the city for a better life. Day in day, day out, they would come by the post office to see if any mail had come for them. It was painful to see the dejection on their face when there is no mail. At times, Charolette was also saddened by the feelings of hurt and disappointment of these parents worrying about their grown children, even knowing fully well they are adults.

Most of the day, Charolette became someone's confidante, counselor, advisor, and friend. She didn't mind at all. Her service to the community was more important and rewarding in many ways. She threw herself into the job with a commitment she had never experienced before. She found herself being excited and anxious to get up in the morning knowing she had something to look forward to being in the post office.

On some days, the highlight of her day would be individuals who just came to talk. And talk. Then she would hear all the gossip, some she could not even repeat in the presence of other neighbors who used the post office on a daily basis. She learned so much from different people who were so kind and generous in encouraging her to strive for great things, but most of all is to do her parents proud. Actually, when some of the neighbors spoke of her parents she could see the sincerity in their countenance, that whatever her parents had done for them, they still had a sense of gratitude.

Charolette knew she had a tough act to follow. She was determined to succeed in being a good citizen of the community along with its responsibilities. She learned how to be silent, not in a disrespectful way, but she did not want to engage in negative conversations about others. And there were plenty who stopped by to engage in negative gossip.

She herself had experienced the effects of negative conversations following her shame and disgrace after having children out of wedlock. The whole community had been in a frenzy about it, and the remarks were painful and emotionally scarred her for a long time. She did not want to do the same to someone else.

Meeting Washington

It was not long after Charolette started working at the post office that her life changed once again. This day, she was working a little late, doing some work she had left over from the day before. She saw this young man walk in.

"Hi," he greeted. "How are you?"

Charolette just nodded but did not pay him much attention as she continued trying to concentrate on what she was doing.

"Hi," he said again in a firmer tone. "Are you always this rude?"

That comment bothered her. She was not in the best of moods that day and she needed to get home to the children. Even though she trusted her brothers Paul and Joshua to feed them, young men did not always see children as a priority. There were plenty of other things they could be doing. Turning to address the person who had spoken, Charolette was in shock and awe.

The person standing there was a gentleman who had just moved into the community. There was talk about him from almost every woman in the community. Charolette wasn't interested at all; her life was finally feeling like she was going somewhere with it so she did not have time to even entertain those types of conversation. It was the strangest feeling. Her heart fluttered and she suddenly felt a giddiness overtake her as if she was a little school girl just getting her first kiss.

"May I help?" she asked.

"What take you so long to answer me?" he responded.

He was a little too cocky for her taste.

"What can I assist you with?" she asked.

"You still don't answer my question," he insisted.

"Sir, I am extremely busy and I don't have time to waste."

"Okay, I'll come another time whenever you have some time to talk to me."

She stood there thinking, "What in God's name this man want from me?" The conversation had caught her off guard and she was also disturbed by his presumptuousness, acting as if he was some kind of gift to women. Then again, when you live in a community where most of the men are married or in their older years, anything will look good to you.

After he left in came the "Village Lawyer" the one who knew everybody's business.

"So, I see you met Washington?" the woman asked as she pulled herself closer.

"Who is Washington?" Charolette asked.

"That nice gentleman who just came out of the post office."

"Listen," Charolette cautioned, "I am not sure what you are trying to get at, but what I can tell you is my focus is far beyond that nonsense."

The Silent Hurt of Charolette Erica Atwell

"Well, my dear, he his single and in demand so you better join the race before he is taken by one of those "floozies" who is doing everything to get his attention."

"Well, that is not my concern. I am not into those foolishness furthermore."

Charolette was raised with too much dignity to subject herself to that type of desperation. Then the woman slyly changed the topic.

"How you and the children's father doing?"

Charolette had been trained to have respect for her elders but this was too much.

"What does that have to do with you?"

"Lord. You don't have to be so touchy about it."

"You are always trying to get in someone else's business."
"Not really," the woman replied. "I am just a person who knows what most of you who act as if you are better than anyone else is doing behind closed doors."

"And what might that be?" Charolette asked in a stern tone.

Realizing that the conversation was getting way out of control, Charolette decided to end it and return to her chores of sorting out the mail for that day. The woman stood there as if she was waiting for Charolette to start another conversation about Washington. A part of her was very upset and more pressing was this burning anger inside her. *How dare this old fool come inquiring about my life when hers is like a storybook within itself?*

Finally, Charolette renewed the courage to ask her why she was so interested in what other people did with their lives.

The Silent Hurt of Charolette Erica Atwell

"I am just a lonely soul waiting for nothing," she explained. "All my life I've been a total failure. Everything that I've ever done was a failed effort. Friends, family, and even my husband turned their backs on me and my husband no longer shows any interest in me."

"That doesn't mean your life is over. It wasn't always that easy for me. Do you find pleasure in making other people unhappy?"

"No I don't, but I think you are one of the nicest young lady from the community. Your parents raised you in such a beautiful way. I know children sometimes stray from the instruction of their parents, but that doesn't mean your life is over. I am not trying to tell you what to do or encouraging you to enter into a relationship that would be detrimental to you. I do believe though with all my heart that you're a suitable candidate for the gentleman because of your upbringing and your family background. Consider what I am saying to you."

Charolette was still not convinced especially because of what she had been through with the children's father. She was not willing in any shape or form to try another relationship while she was still in a state of depression. She was still hurting from all that had happened.

"Charolette," the woman said as she turned to leave, "there isn't much this community has to offer with regards to a suitable man, and so if you have the opportunity, don't let it slip through your hands."

"I am not interested in that right now," Charolette protested. "There are too many issues to deal with right now and my priority is in a different place."

The Silent Hurt of Charolette Erica Atwell

As the woman left, Charolette realized how much time they had spent in conversation. The day had slipped by and she had not completed her work. She was already exhausted from the conversation so she decided to finish her work the next day, first thing in the morning.

On her way home on that long walk down the hill, she couldn't help but think about the conversation she had earlier that day. She had stopped at the shop earlier on to get some cold medicine. She felt like she was coming down with something. She could not afford to be sick at this time.

The conversation was pressing on her mind and it lay heavily on her heart.

"Charolette, how are you?" the storekeeper greeted. "You are doing such a wonderful job at the post office. Thank you for getting my mail to me in a timely manner. How are the children?"

"They are fine," Charolette replied.

"I have something for you so don't leave. I was hoping when you were passing by I would have seen you so just hold on a minute."

While Charolette waited for the shopkeeper to return, she could not help replaying the conversation in her head. Was there even a possibility that her life could change this way? Was this man going to be a part of her future? After all, she did have two children already.

When the storekeeper returned, he gave Charolette a big bag.

"Take this home for you and the children. Your parents were great people and I am forever indebted to them. When I was in difficulties they assisted me so it's only fair now that I do just a little to show my appreciation for all that they have done."

Charolette took the bags and started her journey towards home. But this Washington idea was taking up a big space in her mind.

She was so happy to finally get home and take off her shoes and rest her tired feet. Most of the day she had done a lot of standing and was just elated to take the time for relaxation. That night, Charolette went to bed feeling peaceful inside.

The next day, she went to work at her usual time to open the post office. There were already two people waiting with mail that they needed to send.

"Just give me a moment and I'll be right there with you." She explained to them. Their mail was urgent, they said.

As she sorted out the mail, Washington showed up.

"Good morning," he greeted. "How are you?"

She had pretended not to see him. With her back turned to him this time she answered in a timely manner:

"I am fine."

"I was trying to talk to you yesterday but you were a little snobbish. Any reason for that?"

"I don't go around entertaining strangers."

"Well, first I must say I am no stranger. My name is Washington and I am not just like everybody else. So what's with all the hostility towards me? I am only trying to make friends."

"There are quite a few other girls around here that you won't find it difficult to make friends with, so I see no reason for you to bother me."

"What if am not interested in other people?"

Charlotte's ears kind of pricked up like a horse ready to run. In her mind she was saying, "Hmm, tell me more."

"I have seen you before and said to myself, 'that is a nice girl and I would definitely like to talk with her if I ever have the opportunity'. Then I started to inquire about you and learned that you are the post mistress so I took the liberty of stopping by."

"So what does that have to do with me?"

"Nothing. It has everything to do with me, I suppose. I need to let you know that, so how can I get to know you better in a different kind of setting? I know you are at your job and definitely not a good place to jeopardize your job. Anyhow, I am staying just down by the road with my grandaunt who is very ill. You see, she needed someone to assist her with her daily chores and her doctor's visits."

When he said that, something moved inside Charolette's stomach. It was a feeling that lasted for a long time; she had never felt it before. There was this smile on his face that brightened the whole office. She felt a sense of passion and care; not like she hadn't experienced passion before, but this was just so different.

A major part of Charolette was also scared of what may happen. She was afraid of giving this relationship a chance; what would be the repercussions or benefits. She had to evaluate every aspect of this possible relationship. Charolette started to feel alive again after a long hiatus

The Silent Hurt of Charolette Erica Atwell

from relationships. Washington brought a sense of hope with each passing day. She was growing fonder of him. His kindness was just so overwhelming.

All of that pent up anger she had inside of her was slowly disappearing and she was feeling more openness to new beginnings with Washington in ways she had never dreamt of before; the possibilities were endless. When Charolette decided to take the relationship one step further, there were some concerns that she had so she sat with him and went over some of them. They were not anything major, but just the few things that would cause the relationship not to work.

Charolette had her fair share of cheating, verbal abuse, and emotional abuse so she was adamant that she was not going down that path again. Washington also had his concerns about commitment. He did not want to be in a relationship just for the fun. Charolette wasn't about to play any games either. She knew what it felt like to be on the receiving end of someone else's game. It was refreshing to hear someone speak so candidly about what they desired from a relationship.

So Charolette and Washington began their relationship. It was not like now when people go on dates and expect something sexual at the end of it. Washington was a gentleman and Charolette was happy that a man wanted to spend time with her without wanting to lift her dress up as the first thing.

Charolette was extremely jealous and protective of what she thought was hers. When all the other young girls in the community chased after Washington, it was frustrating and sometimes nerve wracking for her. Those desperate

The Silent Hurt of Charolette Erica Atwell

fools were so rude and blatantly disrespectful that sometime she felt like she just would snatch some of them and slap the silliness out of them. They were outright rude and showing signs of desperation. It was understandable; he was a gorgeous gentleman, tall and handsome from a family who apparently had raised him well to have some kind of courtesy to women. That was fascinating to Charolette.

He was never someone to walk around feeling as if he was God's gift to women, but had this sweet, humble spirit about him. Washington walked with his head held high and had this presence about him that was hard to resist. That, perhaps, was one of his major flaws that left Charolette feeling insecure and thinking that he would leave her when he found someone more attractive than she was or who did not have any children. Washington always reassured her how much he loved her. He came home in the evening at the time he said he would be home.

They went for long walks on the mountainside, just enjoying the beauty of the island and each other's company. They were inseparable from the moment they decided to give the relationship a try. Charolette had wanted that comfort for a long time and longed for the day when she would feel so loved and cherished. Thinking back to her previous relationship, it seemed like another lifetime ago. If she did not have her two children, it would be like it had never existed.

She clung to this man with every part of her being to make sure they survived all the outside elements of women who were constantly trying to gain his attention. They weathered the stormy days by reminding themselves why they were together and it was pretty simple. They would

The Silent Hurt of Charolette Erica Atwell

always tell each other of their love; they would hold hands and embrace each other; just doing the simple things that made a difference. There were no secrets or unkind words spoken to each other. Anything that affected one of them would be talked about honestly and openly. This process worked enormously well for them; it set their minds at ease knowing they were honest about everything that happened in their life on a daily basis. They shared their hurts, pains, disappointments, struggles and challenges.

After a while Washington and Charolette were at a point where they wanted to improve their lives. They had outgrown the rural part of the island and it was time for them to move on. The job situation had not improved; if anything, it was now worse and most of the younger people were moving away in search of better opportunities. Working the land did not seem like something anyone wanted to do anymore. Charolette and Washington had been thinking about it for quite some time but had never really got around to making any commitments. His grandaunt was still very much dependent on him and she had no one else should Washington leave the community.

The rural part of the Island had become extremely difficult to survive. It was not only the young people who were leaving; there were families who were pulling up roots and leaving for a better way of life or to fulfill their educational dreams. Being a farming community, most of, if not all of the money earned and spent within the community was from farming the lands. It was no longer feasible for them to just exchange crops with each other to ensure that everyone had enough to eat. Things and times were changing and the needs of people with it. It was more than keeping their bellies full. Money became necessary as part of daily life to get them the things they needed to live a more comfortable life.

More and more things were just at a point of desperation for some and for others they were just going through the motions of surviving another day. Washington had stopped working, so there was no other income other than Charolette's earnings from her job at the post office. Before, it was only about herself and her children and her brothers now old enough to fend for themselves somewhat. Now, with another mouth to feed, Charolette felt like she was moving backwards in time. The kids were growing up nicely and were going to school. She wanted to give them a better future than what seemed to be awaiting them right now. She believed that, as their parent, it was her responsibility to give them the greatest opportunity that she could afford or able in order for them to succeed.

Washington was very adamant about leaving the rural part of the island. He had his reservation about moving to the city, not only because of his responsibility to his grandaunt, but also because all he had really known was farming and he had great skills in cultivating the land. His concerns were valid and Charolette had the same fears herself. She had never even been to the city and the prospect of having to live there was daunting.

There were people who had left for the city to experience a better way of life but who had to come back worst off than before. It was like a jungle out there, they said, a jungle made of concrete. They had moved with dreams of accomplishing more than they ever could in the rural area. Many had been disappointed. Furthermore, it was not as simple as packing up and saying, "let's go and seek

The Silent Hurt of Charolette Erica Atwell

success!" Washington had the notion of the bitterness and competitive agenda of people in the city and he was scared that he wouldn't measure up to those he came into contact with. Charolette's whole concept was that they had to do the right things in giving an opportunity to themselves and the children, and approach it with positive minds. "Nothing tried, nothing done", was a famous expression of most of the older folk.

For Charolette, life had become hard and miserable, even though she and Washington had a wonderful relationship. A part of her was sure that she would be able make some kind of head way in the city and she was willing to go the extra mile at whatever cost. She was ready to take the chance in the big city where opportunities awaited rather than confine herself to a small space, the community where she had spent all her life.

Charolette would never criticize her upbringing or the people who had played a major role in her life. It was the same community she was in a rush to get out of that had taught her many lessons from which she had learned. It was not that she was being ungrateful. Charolette wasn't a person who ran around and complained about her situation whether good or bad. But, all around, a lot of the old shops and stores she had known all her life were closing. Some, of the people had passed; the children were not interested in continuing what their parents had started. The economy and the difficulties in sustaining the changing dynamics of younger generations whose aspirations and dreams didn't have anything to do with farming, but more on the verge of achieving goals their parent's never attain, was taking its toll on the small communities all across the island.

The Silent Hurt of Charolette Erica Atwell

The Post Office had become even more difficult to maintain for the simple fact that the number of letters which were sent in previous years from overseas and other parts of the island started to dwindle drastically. Charolette knew that something had to be done to pull herself and her family out of the place they were slowly sliding into. With so many people returning home and painting a bleak picture of what life was like in the city for those who had been left behind, Charolette was a bit torn. However, she was still determined to go and experience the ups and downs for herself. She had reached a point in her life when she said to herself, "Enough is enough. If I don't do it now, I don't know if I will get the courage to do it again."

They started to discuss the possibility of moving to the city in a more meaningful and constructive way and not so much the negative aspect of city life and relocating.

Relocation is never an easy thing to do; you're always walking into the unknown no matter how you think you can handle or adjust to the changes. Charolette was able to convince Washington that the best option for her was to move for a good cause. Before they made a final decision, there were some stipulations attached to the process. Washington in a calm demeanor finally said:

"Charolette, promise me that if we move to the city and nothing is working well for us, we'll pack our stuff and return home."

Charolette was so excited to hear him say that they were at least giving it a chance. That was all it was: giving it a chance in terms of trying something new with their lives. They would either succeed or not. Charolette responded to

Washington with such joy. Hearing him in his cool and calm voice saying he was willing to try was totally a confirmation of her persistence in convincing him to move to the city.

The best thing to do was to have a definite time frame when they wanted to move and where they were going to stay. Washington was always a man of character who prided himself in standing up and doing everything possible for his family. He did not like crowds; loved the country life; never had many friends. But, he knew what he had to do. Charolette was hoping to go the city and get a job as a postmistress or even something similar. With the experience she had, she was extremely optimistic about finding a job.

It was agreed that they would give it the best possible chance of succeeding while at the same time they were planning their exit strategy. The decision process was long and hard. If things didn't work out, they could always return home. The key was when to decide that is was time to return to the country.

So off they went on their new journey as a family with the little that they had and everything they could carry to sustain them for a period of time. Paul and Joshua would stay behind to mind the house. They were both now old enough to manage themselves.

One of Charolette's favorite aunts was living in the city and would often come to the country during the holidays. She was always dressed up and glamorous in beautiful dresses and jewelry. Her conversation was always about how the city was so wonderful and she had made herself successful at what she did as a nurse.

The Silent Hurt of Charolette Erica Atwell

Charolette asked herself how difficult can it be because if her aunt could do it then she also had the ability to accomplish some of the things she talked about. She was all psyched up for this new chapter or phase in her life. So the arrangement was made with her aunt and it was confirmed that they could stay with her until they were able to go out on their own. It was not always easy living with family. There were all these idiosyncrasies that could make it a real challenge. Secretly, Charolette worried about how her aunt would be able to accommodate them all.

But her aunt assured her it wouldn't be a problem. Charolette did not like imposing on anyone, more so her aunt. She did not want her to feel uncomfortable in her own home, especially with two children running around her feet. If it were just her and Washington, they could easily make themselves small. Children did not understand that notion. But they had no choice as they moved forward to start their new life. What the future held for them, they did not know. They just knew that they had to try something. They could not continue living in the poverty that was overtaking them in the community that had shaped their lives.

The Silent Hurt of Charolette Erica Atwell

Living in the Capital

On the day they arrived in the city, it was sunny and beautiful like a promise. It was a totally different scenery from what Charolette had grown up with in the rural part of the Island. The hustling and bustling was quite evident; everyone was just moving at a fast pace with bus and car horns blaring.

They got off the bus exactly where her aunt had told them to and there she was, standing there waiting patiently. She was obviously elated to see them. However, even with all the assurance from her aunt, Charolette still felt a small fear raising its ugly head again. There were other family members there waiting on their loved ones also. It seemed some of the people had the same idea and were running away from their circumstance for a better way of life in the city.

Charolette hugged her aunt tightly and kissed her while she whispered in her ear:

"Thank you for your kindness. It means a great deal to me. I hope I'll be able to return the favor to you someday." "Don't worry," she gently whispered, "that is what families are for. We do take care of each other."

In that moment Charolette's spirit was calm and at peace knowing at least she would have somewhere to lay her head with Washington and the children. Getting to her house wasn't a long journey; it was within walking distance. This was a different world for Charolette. There were street lights, fences, handcarts, bars with loud music playing, and folks were just sitting on the sidewalks doing nothing.

The Silent Hurt of Charolette Erica Atwell

They arrived at her aunt's house. It wasn't this great big mansion that Charolette imagined but it was a beautiful home just looking at it from the outside. The inside was pretty decent and clean; everything was in order. The accommodation was there, even though it was going to be a little bit tight, but Charolette was excited to start her new life in the city.

Washington never really said much. He had always been a man of few words except for that first time he had declared his intentions toward her. His silence sometimes left Charolette frustrated since it was not always easy to guess what he was thinking. As he looked around him at their new abode, Washington turned to Charolette's aunt with this stoic look on his face.

"I am forever grateful to you for opening up your home and allowing us to stay here with you. We pray that our time here will be short and not to put a burden on you, but make every effort to assist you in any way we can."

Charolette was shocked at his openness. Maybe the city was going to be good for him, after all. That was one of the first times she had ever seen Washington in such a spirit of gratitude and humility, just showing his human side, and never really caring about being vulnerable. Her aunt was even more humble to assist her niece.

"You are family," she replied, "and if we need help, it is our duty to be of some assistance to each other in any which way we can, so don't worry about it. You'll do just fine."

Charolette and her aunt went into the kitchen to prepare food for the family. After such a long journey on the bus, they were hungry, but more excited about being in the city.

The Silent Hurt of Charolette Erica Atwell

After all, they had heard so much about this wonderful part of the island.

However, in the short space of time being there, Charolette was not that impressed with what she had seen so far. She thought it would be more of this great city where everybody had this great career or job. It wasn't like the rural part of the island where houses were far apart with huge land spaces with trees and the cool afternoon breeze. The houses were all joined together and look congested, so Charolette asked her aunt why people live in such close proximity to each other.

"This is what they call a tenement yard where people share space with each other," she replied. "Welcome to the real world, my child. But it is not that bad as it seems. You have to have that zeal to want to make a good way of life. Take the initiative to think big and strive for great things."

The next morning they rose to a new day. Her aunt was already getting ready for work. She had come to the city a long time ago and done pretty well for herself. She had gone to school and became a nurse. Her aunt was in a place of comfort in contrast to the rest of the community; in fact, most of the residents weren't doing as well. Charolette was in awe of her success, at times hoping the day would come when she too would be able to achieve a fraction of what her aunt had accomplished. It was not like she was feeling any form of jealousy, but the thought of being in a position of independence was significant. Charolette's intentions were definitely purposeful and focused in the sense of taking all the necessary precautions to map out her future in this new environment.

The Silent Hurt of Charolette Erica Atwell

With all the congestion, hustling, and bustling, every day seemed like every single person you came across was in a hurry to go somewhere, whereas in the rural part of the island people were more relaxed and easy going. Soon, Charolette got caught up in the daily chores of living in the city. She was not used to the fast paced environment but in order to succeed she would have to definitely move with the flow of things to the point where she was in a state of confusion. Understanding the whole dynamics of city life was a challenge in every aspect of surviving the daily chaos of the overpopulated city in terms of density.

Finally, she was in full flight, understanding the concept of what worked and what did not. She learned to apply the few skills she observed and taught herself along the way. Making a decent living within the confines of the city wasn't all that it was hyped up to be; it was a difficult process and tiresome. Many times on the bus going to her day job she would overheard all kinds of conversation about bosses and how awful some of them were. In Charolette's mind she had always learned to adapt to situations she could not control or have no business trying to change people who have been that way all their lives. Work was important to her in providing for herself and family.

Washington found little odd jobs here and there. He also was a frugal individual who watched every penny. He would explain the significance of leaving the rural part of the island and was absolutely sure that he would never be a statistic of the city. By the look of things, you could easily get caught up and by the time you realize it you are in deep depression just trying to get by on the little you have accumulated.

The Silent Hurt of Charolette Erica Atwell

It wasn't long after that Charolette found out she was pregnant again. This would be the first child from the union between Washington and Charolette. By then Jacob and his sister Sandra were going to school in the city and were no longer underfoot.

Washington was extremely excited and looking forward to his first child. He went into overdrive. He took jobs that he normally wouldn't just to make sure that when the baby was born they would have ample enough to sustain them. Charolette began to grow fonder of him seeing his commitment to his family. He reminded her of her father and his drive to see his family comfortable. Washington worked long hours and sometimes came home very late at night. Charolette worried for his safety and prayed to God that nothing would happen to him on his way home from working to provide for his family. Her aunt was still very supportive and never one day showed any kind of disdain towards them. She made sure everything was in order for them to feel at home.

Charolette and Washington were laying down one summer night. It was extremely hot and muggy outside. They could hear the sounds of people chatting and laughing, just about everything. Washington and Charolette were never ones to socialize that much anyhow so it was customary for them to just share with each other. After a while, the conversation got intense, not in a bad way, but they were discussing the topic of moving to their own little place for the simple fact there was a baby on the way and they needed to have some sense of dignity living in her aunt's house. With three children, the place would soon become overcrowded and it was not fair to her aunt.

Charolette had learned a little sewing from her mother. It was necessary then for all young women to be able to sew a seam or be able to do some embroidery. Charolette felt it was time to put her unused skills to work for her.

One evening, her aunt came home and was ecstatic about a good connection she had with the man she was seeing at the time. He knew some people who could get Washington a job working in one of the major companies in the city. Washington's face registered the thought of a burden being lifted from his shoulder. He went for the interview and got the job.

Now it was time for the family to think about where they were going to live. They had to do something before the baby was born. Charolette did not want to move to another place where they had to share the basic facilities with strangers. She did not think it was a good thing for her children Jacob and Sandra to be playing with some of the children that could be found in the tenement yard. Her parents would have a fit if they knew that their grandchildren were 'mixing up' like that. With a new child, it was imperative that they changed their way of living.

They went on a search to find a decent way to enhance their future. In the meantime, they both had to work in order to survive. They rose early for work each morning and returned late in the evening in time to get the children fed, spend a little time with them, and then send them off to bed.

Charolette's aunt was proud of her niece, even though she never said it. In comparison to many other people who had left the country for the city, Charolette and Washington were doing very well. Too many had become victims in the sense of not applying themselves and making use of opportunities for success.

Charolette's stomach was growing. Washington's main concern was for her to have the smoothest pregnancy; he was extremely attentive and caring and never showed any signs of resentment. Charolette stayed home and became a housewife to the children and Washington. She loved him more than she could imagine loving a man. Life had become more attainable for them and their dreams seemed to be coming true.

One beautiful evening as the sun was going down, they were sitting talking about the blessings and favor of God and how he had allowed them to experience something that they never thought possible.

"Charolette," Washington said in his serious tone, "there is nothing more that I would like to do than make you my wife."

The tears fell down Charolette's face. She was in a state of shock and disbelief. Her heart was pounding and she was so overwhelmed with joy and fear, joy in the sense that this was what she had always wanted. If only her parents were here to see this moment. Why had she not met this man before? She was happy for the blessings of her children and she would not give them up for all the love in the world; but her life would have been so much easier if she had met Washington first.

Fear of the unknown is always a joy stealer. Because of the uncertainty bottled up inside of her, she began asking herself all kinds of questions. Washington held her hand and assured her it was going to be alright. Charolette's heart stopped pounding and she felt this sweet sense of belonging. They sat with her aunt and let her know their intentions. It was the right thing to do after all that she had done for them.

They started to plan the wedding; it would have to be after the baby was born. So the wheel was in motion and they were both excited.

One day while she was alone at home, Charolette began experiencing sharp pains. It was not yet time for her to have the baby so she was a little concerned that this baby might come too early. Babies born prematurely did not have a good chance of surviving. Her pain was excruciating. Even though Charolette already had two children, for some reason she was in unimaginable pain that she had never felt before. She called the neighbor to come and assist in getting her to the hospital. Her aunt had told her that if she ever needed help she could always call on the neighbor.

They arrived at the hospital in a reasonable amount of time. During the ride to the hospital, the pain never eased for a moment. Labor pains would sometimes take a break, she knew; but this felt different. Charolette was checked in but after that, she could not recall what happened. She woke up a few hours later; there were doctors standing all around her with clipboards, and discussing her diagnosis. Most of the medical terminology they were using she did not have a concept of what it meant or how to decipher the actual meaning. At one point, she opened her eyes and Washington and her aunt were at her bedside. They looked at her as if they were seeing a ghost.

The doctors explained that she had an ectopic pregnancy and was lucky to be alive. The baby had become lodged in one of her tubes and, while it was growing, it had come to a point where the tube could not expand anymore and was getting ready to burst. They had to remove the fetus since it could not survive under those conditions. Charolette herself could die if the pregnancy continued. They had no choice but to terminate it.

Washington was devastated and went into a mode of depression for quite a while. The thought of losing Charolette was overwhelming; but there was the other pain of losing the child they had made together. Charolette assured him that everything was going to be alright and that they would definitely try again, so there is no need for him to get sad or disappointed. It was a hard one to swallow but they had to move on with the pain.

Their attention then became focused on the wedding. Charolette went into overdrive mode as she tried to bury the pain of losing her child. Although they did not have much, Charolette was determined to make this her dream come true wedding. She loved this man so much; he had been so good to her and she did not intend to marry anyone else for as long as she lived. This was it; Washington was the only man she wanted to spend the rest of her life with.

Their wedding day ceremony was beautiful and special; it was everything Charolette had planned for and dreamed of. The whole ambiance was so mellow and peaceful and they had a wonderful time with family and friends.

The one drawback was that Jacob and Sandra were not too happy about it. Washington had been like a father to them and some people did not even know that he was not their real father. However, somehow they believed it meant that their own father would be banned from their lives. It was strange because they had not seen much of him since leaving the country and he was not playing much of a role in their lives.

Washington and Charolette were inseparable. They tried to do things as a couple; he was a phenomenal person whom she loved and adored. There was no way Charolette was going to give up the happiness she had found with Washington for a man who had not been there for her and her children when she need him. Charolette was committed to explain to her children the significance of being with Washington.

Washington was just working long hours trying to provide for the family in any way possible. They didn't even have time for a vacation and even if they wanted to, financially they couldn't afford it so they learned to do with what they had. At times, they would sit and talk or more like daydream of what it would be like going on a cruise or some other place where the sun shone beautifully.

Each day brought on new challenges and a little bit more success for Charolette and Washington. They finally found somewhere that they could call home and with the help of her aunt they were able to move into their own home. It was a relief and a huge accomplishment for them. Washington was doing pretty well at his job and working his way up the ladder. The opportunities came fast and quick. Washington was always an individual who had to be told or shown it once and that was it; he could function on his own independently. They were glad they decided to move to the city.

The Silent Hurt of Charolette Erica Atwell

Washington was extremely gifted in terms doing things around the house fixing and patching up things, so when they moved in and there was a lot of work to be done, he took on each task with ease. On his day off he would work all day into evening making sure everything was precise and in its rightful place. Charolette's role in all of this was to make sure he had eaten because if she allowed him to he would go all day without a bite to eat.

Their home became a place of peace and serenity to the point where sometimes she thought it was too quiet.

At nights before going to bed Charolette would pray and ask God, "Why am I not having children for this wonderful man who you have sent me?" She came to the realization that it probably was not going to happen, and she would just have to live with the fact that she would not bear any children for him. They went on about their daily lives. Washington never really entertained the conversation about Charolette having children for him; maybe he was afraid of the same results as before.

Sometimes Charolette's thoughts took control of her with ridiculous ideas of him leaving her because she could not give him a child. Somewhere in all of the challenges that they were facing, she found out that she was pregnant. This was a time in her life where she had given up on having any more children so she kept it a secret and never told Washington. A part of her was afraid that she would build up his hopes and then he would be crushed going through what they had been through previously. The puzzling thing was that she became pregnant at a point in life where she thought it couldn't have happened anymore. At her age, having a child was a risky endeavor.

The Silent Hurt of Charolette Erica Atwell

Anyhow, she kept the pregnancy to herself. She did not want to get excited and have the same meltdown she had before. On one occasion, her aunt stopped by the house just to see how they were doing. She was always loving and caring so it did not surprise or annoy Charolette one bit that she would check up on them. Family was important to both of them.

Charolette was standing in the kitchen making dinner when she heard:

"Charolette, are you pregnant?" in her aunt's well-spoken voice.

Forgetting that her aunt was a nurse, Charolette quickly responded:

"No, Aunt!"

"Why you are lying to me?" she demanded in a more stern voice.

"Aunt, I am scared of what will happen if I should lose this child. I don't want to build up my hopes and be disappointed in not having the baby."

"Did you talk to Washington about it?"

"No I did not. Ever since I had lost the baby, he hasn't said much, so I don't want to build up his hopes and then what occurred before happen again. I know he would be devastated so I am kind of keeping it a secret."

"Charolette, you know he will eventually find out. Then what are you going tell him? You just have to build the courage and talk with him because if it's God's will, nothing can stop it."

The Silent Hurt of Charolette Erica Atwell

Charolette felt a sense of peace that she never felt before. It gave her some reassurance that it was going to be alright and she should stop being so worried about things she really didn't have any control over.

After that, she and her aunt sat in the kitchen and talked about her childhood and all that had happened until then. It was like strolling down memory lane. Her aunt assured her that everything was going to be alright and whatever help she needed she'd be there to assist. They ate the meal around the table and right there and then all the fears Charolette had subsided. As the conversation progressed, it was like a part of her was re-born.

Before she left, her aunt asked:

"Do you need anything?"

"No, Aunt. You have done so much for us. There is nothing more you can give that you haven't already given."

"That is not your concern to dictate to me what I should do."

Deep down inside Charolette was thinking: I wonder if this lady knows I am a grown woman, not a child. Why is she talking to me like I am her child? Then it hit her: her aunt never had any children. She had taken care of Charolette and her siblings for so long, especially after their parents died; she was the one who took on the role of parenting.

Before she left, she gave Charolette a sealed envelope with her name on it. Charolette hugged her and told her thanks and whispered in her ear, "I love you more than you ever know." She held on tight.

"Don't worry, you'll be alright," her aunt promised.

The Silent Hurt of Charolette Erica Atwell

So Charolette started to build up the courage to tell Washington the good news of her pregnancy, hoping he would accept the fact that they were finally going to have a baby. Washington was always a quiet type. It seemed nothing ever really bothered him so she wasn't sure how he would react to the news. Deep down inside she was also worried that she would jinx the pregnancy by telling him. Her plan was to wait until he found out on his own.

When he came home from work, he looked at Charolette and said:

"Are you alright?"

"Yes," she assured him.

"You just look a little tired."

"Today I had just rough day doing the house chores. For some reason I was just feeling a little melancholy in my spirit."

Washington thought she was referring to the current situation because he had high hopes of moving into a more exclusive part of city; he would do everything in his power to make sure they achieved that goal.

"I know what you're thinking," she said to him, "you don't have to worry about that. We'll make the best of what we have as long as we are focused on doing the right thing. What I really want to talk to you about is my pregnancy."

"What?" he responded.

The look on his face was priceless. He smiled and the whole room brightened with his joy. Charolette felt the love like she had never felt before. Washington hugged her tightly; he was definitely looking forward to having his first child. They sat down and talked about it for a while, just discussing all the possibilities, hoping this time it would go well, in terms of the birth of the baby.

On the day Charolette was due to have the baby, Washington wasn't home. Her aunt hadn't gone to work that day and her oldest, Jacob was home. So when Charolette started to feel the pain and cramps, she knew then it was time. She asked Jacob to go and call her aunt. Then she waited for a little while enduring the pains that she had never felt before, even during her two previous pregnancies. There was just something about this pregnancy. On top of that, she was worried that something would go wrong like it had the last time. Her aunt came in a hurry but, by the time she got there Charolette was almost at the stage where the baby was about to born. Her aunt put on her nurse's hat, hypothetically speaking, and started with helping to deliver the baby.

A beautiful girl came out screaming at the top of her lungs. When Washington came home from work and saw her, he just stood there with tears in his eyes, crying uncontrollable at the mere fact that he had given up hope of having any children. Charolette was also excited knowing the bond that they had would grow even stronger.

Washington became extra attentive for the rest of the evening and Charolette loved every second of it. The feelings were just too great not to bask in the opportunity of having a man with such compassion. So they raised their daughter Olivia in a stable home with love.

Two years after that, Charolette became pregnant again. At a stage in her life where she considered herself up in age, it scared the living daylights out of her. After Olivia was born and she had gone to the hospital for a visit to make sure everything was okay, the doctors had sat her down and spoke to her about the risk of getting pregnant at a time when you're considered up in age, the damage to child can be severe. So when she found out she was pregnant again, all of that flashed through her mind and it was extremely frightening.

They sat down as they always did and Charolette told him the good news. He was excited again. Then she reminded him of the last conversation she had with the doctors that kind of brought him down to reality. They looked at each in a way that was somewhat joyous and a sense of heartbreak; emotions were mixed and the question would be what their best options were.

This time the birth wasn't painful as the one before. Everything went well during the pregnancy and the actual birth. The doctors this time were more persuasive in reminding her that, this was it and she should take all the necessary precautions not to get pregnant again. The house was filled with joy and love and each day brought new challenges. But they were able to weather all of them in manner that most people only dreamed of. In the back of their minds, the family was completed with the addition of baby Richard.

Jacob and Sandra were still angry over the fact that their mother had married Washington. But she was adamant that they wouldn't steal her joy or take the one true love she had ever had. They would never understand the love she and Washington shared.

Later on, Charolette found out that even her aunt, whom she loved and adored, was also against her marrying

Washington. She thought Charolette could have done better. When Charolette finally discovered the truth, she felt like a part of her had been ripped out. As a matter of fact, the entire side of her family was up in arms over it. They had really thought she was way too good for him, despite the fact that she had two children out of wedlock, and that she should have pursued a career before getting married and having any more children. They treated him with disdain for so long and she was blind to all of the rhetoric that they were spewing behind her back.

As long as Charolette and Washington were together, he never responded to their attitudes and behaviors, acting as if they did not exist. It was like that for many years. Washington's skin was thick and he never talked about it. He was a man of character who loved and adored his family.

George Washington Atwell never really grew up with his biological parents. His father died at a young age; right after that, his mother died. He was raised by aunts and uncles so being in a secure relationship meant everything to him. Over the years Charolette and Washington learnt to block the negative voices and the naysayers. They couldn't allow that kind of behavior to dictate the rest of their lives. They had a purpose to fulfill all that they had set out to achieve.

Things were really starting to look great for them as a family. Charolette had started to do some dressmaking from home. Funny enough how that happened. Washington and Charolette were lying in bed talking one night and she had mentioned that she can sew a little bit. A week later he showed up with a sewing machine in a van and said with his always uncanny smile:

The Silent Hurt of Charolette Erica Atwell

"This is for you. If that's what you want to do, go ahead, design some of the best dress."

Just by sewing dresses and hemming up pants and shirt for the community, Charolette became known to almost everybody within the confines of the community in which they lived. There was always a part of her who wanted to take a different approach in the affairs of the community, what they were entitled to and how it was distributed. Most of the houses were in dilapidated condition and in dire need of fixing. The roads were just treacherous: no street lights, water was a scarce commodity, the basic needs of the people just weren't been met by the so called politicians.

She started to do some research on the roles and responsibility of the government at that time and found out there were ways the people could get some assistance from the government to help with their current situation. The first person she recruited was Washington and she outlined all the initiatives to help them move forward in getting the help for the people of the community. So Charolette took on the task with great pride going to every possible meeting/function that was held all over the city found out who she needed to speak with or discuss the ramification of not providing the necessary service of the community he represented.

They started a little group called "Conqueror of the South West Branch." Their main focus was to mobilize people to take their destiny into their own hands and demand what was rightfully theirs. The organization grew in numbers. They were a force to reckon with in that part of the city. The Member of Parliament became more attentive to their needs and concerns. A lot of things were being done to elevate the living conditions that existed at that time.

Work was allocated for the community on a regular basis. Information was passed on where and when there was job opening, and the Farm Worker Programs, School Assistance Program and every other little entitlement program was made known to the people. They had become very successful at what they did for their community. The difference was obvious in the community over a period of time. People were more inclined to achieve and look outside the box; they understood the significance of taking the responsibility for the betterment of their children future. Politically, they were connected. On any given day, Charolette wouldn't be surprised if some politicians wanting to win votes or looking to be on the right side of his constituency would show up at their meeting. But things soon began taking a turn in the city.

After a while, things had become volatile in the city. The political landscape had changed and it became an all-out war among the people living within close proximity to each other. There was hurt, pain, and re-location for some. Unfortunately, Charlotte's family was one of those who had to make a hasty retreat to a different part of the island for safety sake, leaving behind a considerable amount of their belongings.

Unfortunately, they ended up in a community with a lot of similarities like the previous one they were running away from. It was extremely difficult for Washington to go to work in the morning. He had to get up much earlier to get the bus; moreover the walk was about half mile long in comparison to where they were living prior to the re-location. The city had become so violent that a lot of the

The Silent Hurt of Charolette Erica Atwell

businesses were starting to close down due to the violence and the lack of security. This took a toll on the job security of Washington and so many others.

Things were starting to get really slow. Washington wasn't working as much as he used to; it was on a case by case basis. Finally, one evening he came home looking very distraught. Charolette got worried knowing him; he was never the person to look so troubled.

"Charolette, I was terminated today with most of my colleagues. Due to the ongoing turmoil, we can't operate to the full capacity until this uprising is subsided. That was the message from the manager," Washington explained, his face looking like the world he knew was ending.

A million things flash through Charlotte's mind at that moment for her children Olivia and Richard. At that point, she knew it was going to be a test of faith in God. The two sat again like they always did and discussed all the possibilities.

They went to bed that night on their knees praying, asking for divine intervention because at that time they were in a state of disbelief and confusion. Just trying process the likelihood of poverty was beyond their comprehension. After Washington lost his job, he never really was the same. Even though he was able to find little jobs here and there, it wasn't enough for him to settle with just getting by. It bothered him immensely.

For a total of one year, Washington did not work. He just couldn't find anything to do; even the odd jobs were slowing down. That is when they started to discuss going back to the country to do some farming. He was good at farming anyhow and the need was great for agriculture.

The Silent Hurt of Charolette Erica Atwell

This was one moment in time from Charolette first laid eyes on Washington that she was in total disagreement with him.

"Let's stick it out. Things will get better," Charolette pleaded with him. "It can't continue like this. Let's build up the courage to fight it out."

He wasn't in *total* disagreement.

"But look at all that I've put forward. One thing I am asking you, Charolette, lets' give this situation at least another two years and if nothing work as we planned, promise me you'll go back to the rural area where you come from and do farming."

A part of Charolette was torn; furthermore, she did not want to go back not achieving what she had set out to become. Secondly, going back to the rural areas would be just like everyone else who tried before her and failed. Charolette's pride wouldn't allow her to. She was contemplating every possible option to make sure she wouldn't subject herself to that embarrassing situation. Knowing some of those people of the community, they would certainly rejoice over her failure, just like they had done to others before her. People can be sometimes treacherous and mean-spirited, using words that sometimes have long lasting effect.

Things and time had become more and more difficult with each passing day in terms of finding food and work; the dressmaking business that Charolette did was basically non-existent; that it is how hard life had become. They were just going through the motions with what they could find to survive. Olivia and Richard were growing beautifully with a lot of potential. Since they were babies,

Charolette had been sheltering them from the elements of society. She made it her responsibility to not allow any of her children to fall victim to their environment so she shielded them with every fiber of her being.

Charolette found other ways to make a living. Buying and selling a little of the everyday necessary items that people would need wasn't making a great deal of money but it was able to sustain them. Young Richard was by her side through it all, selling plastic bags and everything else he could manage to help them make ends meet. Although it was a sad situation, it helped to bring Charolette and her son closer together. Many evenings they would hop on the bus together at the end of the day with their slim pickings, hoping it would serve them for at least one day. He never left her out as she stayed up late after making sure the family was fed, her feet tired and her eyes barely staying open.

Then something changed. Fortunately, one of Charolette's nieces, one of her brother's daughters residing in Canada, called one night to see how Charolette was doing. Charolette had not spoken with her in some time so it was a surprise to hear from her. She had not spoken to either of her brothers in quite a while too. They talked for a time; then her niece said, "Would you like to come to Canada for a visit?"

At first Charolette was flabbergasted, not knowing what to say.

"Auntie, are you there?"

"Yes, my dear," she responded.

With tears flowing down her eyes, she quietly whispered, "I am so thankful." The reason she was so emotional is that

The Silent Hurt of Charolette Erica Atwell

it was the time she was really in the process of surrendering and going back to the rural part of the island. Charolette shared the good news with Washington that night when he came home from the construction site where he had found temporary employment.

Financial Hardship

Life had become more difficult in many ways. Washington was extremely worried about Charolette leaving him on his own with the children, not knowing how he would survive with no family members or friends to assist him in the event he needed help. Every penny they earned started to be put aside, a small amount for the trip or even more so she could leave with Washington to keep him for a little time until she was able to send home some money.

He was very troubled in his spirit. It was quite evident that there were some things on his mind. Charolette would catch him staring at her with this look of apathy. She assured him what she was going for is a better way of life for them, to elevate their standard of living. He wasn't a jealous kind of gentleman. His concern was more about the children's well-being. So they went into the one thing they always knew to comfort each other. They talked openly about the issue facing them even though he wasn't a guy of many words, but in circumstances or when crisis arose he would speak with authority about the unity of his family. Charolette admired that side of him with compassion and love, knowing she had a friend and husband who would battle through the rough edges of life with her no matter what the circumstances were.

Charolette was optimistic about her invitation to Canada. It was an opportunity at the right time when she needed it most. For that she was excited. Everything was in place for her to leave. She got her two eldest children and the last two together. They sat around the dinner table and she explained to them the situation about her leaving for a better way of life and that it would be beneficial to all of them. To her eldest, Jacob and Sandra, she asked that they would not abandon their brother and sister in her absence and that they would be there in case Washington needed assistance with providing for them going to work. They agreed.

The day Charolette was supposed to leave the island, a part of her was so torn. Leaving Washington on his own was a burden on her heart and very stressful. Eventually, she had to decide between staying on the island and immigrating to Canada for a better way of life.

It was a chilly evening as she made her way to the airport. Much wasn't been said while travelling in the neighbor's car, but you could feel the emotional hurt and uncertainty in Washington.

"Honey, it will be alright," she assured him. "I promise you if it's not conducive to a better way of life for me or stressful, I'll be back within a month."

Arriving in Canada, it was a much different scenery and more modernized in comparison to the island. Charolette was taken aback looking at all those huge buildings and people just hustling and bustling along their way to work or whatever else. She had thought the city was huge and busy when they had moved from the rural area of her island. Everything was so much busier than she could ever imagine. The good thing was that people were not all forced to struggle in a tenement yard.

After Charolette had settled in for a week or so, she had a rude awakening from her niece. What she had initially promised her prior to leaving the island was a far cry from what she was experiencing.

Charolette woke up one morning and was bombarded with all these chores to do inside the house. She was in a state of shock and awe. Not that she expected to come and do nothing; but in the manner which it was presented she felt like she was a house maid rather than a family member. She took the instruction knowing deep down in her heart she wasn't going to subject herself to that kind of abuse; furthermore, her niece was very rude. She liked to talk down to people.

The children were sweet and kind, loving, but were craving attention. Apparently, their mother had been working so many long hours she never found time to spend with her children. Her husband had divorced her because of unethical behavior on both of their parts; they were just living a life of deception. The children were the ones who suffered immensely, craving for both of their attention. They had started to act out in school, which was in direct correlation to what was going on at home. At that point, Charolette knew her purpose was way more significant than she had thought, so she took on the role of just being there for the children with their homework, cleaning the house, and making dinner.

Charolette's niece never seemed to accept her efforts. There was always something to find fault about. Once Charolette sat with her and explicitly asked what she really wanted from her. Her niece went off in a temper tantrum, cursing, swearing and using profanity in the most disgraceful manner. Charolette sat there looking at her with a sense of confusion not knowing how to respond. She was just frightened of her actions. After a while the young woman calmed down and started to cry over her behavior and apologized for her actions, saying that is not her; she didn't know what happened why she had that outburst.

From there on in Charolette knew she had to make some kind of exit strategy which may be available to her at that time. She was willing to put up with a lot in order for her to achieve the ultimate goal of providing for her own family back home.

Washington wasn't doing too well back home; he had given up on a lot of things and was just going through the motions. Each time Charolette called him, she would assure him that her intentions are family oriented and whatever she was doing it is for them and the family. She could see the fear of losing his wife to the elements of society. It was not like Washington was a jealous kind of guy, but he was a humble person with so much love to give and they were a match made in heaven. Charolette not being there caused somewhat of an anxiety.

Six months passed and the abusive behavior continued. Her niece was not paying her for all the services she was performing. She basically was working for free. Charolette sent Washington a letter explaining her current dilemma. Tears flowed down her cheeks as she penned the letter, telling him how much she regretted coming to a foreign land and going through what she going through. Her situation was extremely hard to fathom. He wrote her back explaining the difficulties he was going through with the children in terms of feeding them because the economy had become difficult; almost everything had dried up on the island. Charolette decided it was time for her to go home to her family.

The Silent Hurt of Charolette Erica Atwell

The mere fact that she was in a place of turmoil and feeling abuse didn't make any sense at all. She would rather be home with her family trying to work things out. So she started the process of leaving. Every little penny that she could gather by just going to the store or buying grocery, she put it aside with plans for her return home on her mind. Washington called her once because she had given him the house phone number with strict instruction only to call her during the day at a certain time.

One afternoon after she had finished her house chores, the phone rang. It was Washington and he was crying on the other end of the line. Charolette's heart skipped many beats in that moment. Oh, my God, what happen now? were the thoughts racing through her mind.

"Charolette, I just can't do this no more. I am planning to go to the rural part of the island. The city has become too difficult to survive. Furthermore, yesterday evening the kids were hungry and I didn't have anything to feed them and Jacob had stopped by the house. I explained to him the plight of the children, and asked him to please help with getting them something to eat. He looked at me and bluntly said he don't have anything to give anybody. I couldn't sit there and watch Olivia and Richard twist in hunger while their stomach was just making these weird sounds. So I decided to go out on the streets to see if I could get something for them to eat. I stopped by the bar at the corner of the road where almost everyone goes to drown their sorrows and pain in drinking. When I got there, your son, whom I had asked for assistance for his brother and sister, was inside their buying everyone drinks and bragging about what he has and how much he makes. Charolette, my heart was broken with pain and hurt knowing he could not help his brother and sister, but find the time to be assisting everyone else."

That was when Charolette knew she had to do something. So that night, she sat waiting on her niece to come home so she could explain to her what her intentions were. She came home at her regular time.

"I would like to talk with you," Charolette said to her.

"I don't have any time for that now," she responded in her usual rude manner.

"Well this is of great importance so I think you should be able to listen to me just for a moment. I am planning to go back home to my family."

Oh, she flew off the handle.

"So you rather go back home to that worthless piece of shit you call a husband, while you could make a better way of life here?"

"First and foremost, you are way out of line referring to Washington in that manner and I am extremely offended."

"I won't apologize for what I just said because it is true. I don't know what you are doing with that uneducated man who can't offer you anything but grief."

"At least he is not like you and your husband who lived a life of deception and immoral behavior."

That was it. She was in a fit of rage when Charolette said that. She threatened to put Charolette out on the street in dead of winter. Her heart sunk. To think that family can be so cruel to each other. The kids woke up and started to defend Charolette, telling her she was wrong talking to Charolette like that.

The Silent Hurt of Charolette Erica Atwell

It was time for her to go back home.

Charolette suggested that she make adequate preparations for the kids to go to school and to take care of them. She tried to talk Charolette out of leaving and promised she would even start to pay her. But there was something in her that wasn't genuine. Charolette wasn't buying the sudden change in behavior.

So Charolette returned home to her family after one year in Canada.

It was a bittersweet reunion. A part of her was torn leaving her family; but the other part of her was confused about returning home to a situation that dire and critical. For the year she went away, coming back seemed different. Being in a foreign land with vast access to a lot of things that wasn't accessible to people back on the island was mind boggling. But when you're exposed to a different way of life and opportunities you tend to compare each with a biased perspective.

After returning home, Charolette came to the realization it is more difficult than she had initially thought. People were suffering at a rapid pace, food was in scarce, and some items were married with each other by the shopkeepers. That was just too much to handle. Olivia and Richard were growing with so much grace and poise. Olivia was attending one of the premier high schools on the island. Richard was doing well in school. Their lives returned to a somewhat normal state.

Washington always had the desire to return to the rural part of the island to do farming so Charolette decided it was time to at least give it a try. They had done everything

The Silent Hurt of Charolette Erica Atwell

they had set out to do. Even though a lot of it hadn't materialized, Charolette felt a sense of satisfaction.

It was one hot summer morning when they began the transition back to their original home in the countryside of the island. It wasn't all that bad; they hadn't brought much with them. They had also lost much in their escape from the violence in their part of the city and had not been able to accumulate too much after that. The economy had become too bad and had pushed Charolette to try her luck on foreign soil. That had helped a little but it was more money they returned with than possessions.

Olivia and Richard were now growing into adulthood and it was tough to move, especially Olivia, to finish up school. It was decided that they would remain with her aunt in the city where they would be able to finish school. Washington was excited about going back home. The joy on his face was just too great. He had never really adapted to the city life.

On their arrival, the community came to greet them like they were celebrities; they felt special. There were those with different views and comments, but in life you're going to experience some of that. It never really bothered either of them. The little Charolette had saved during her visit to Canada was helpful in getting them a start. The house had become run down since Joshua had left and Paul was not very good at keeping up the place. Washington was very good with his hands so most the work done on the house was completed by him with the help of the men in the community. From there on, they lived their lives in such peace.

The Silent Hurt of Charolette Erica Atwell

The land was vast and fertile so they planted all kinds of provision to sell. Charolette recalled how her father loved the land. He had worked it with such pride up until his death. Now, here was Washington, with some help from Paul, making the land produce again. She had really married a man after her father's heart. They were able to sell some of their produce to people who came down once per week to purchase items to sell at the market in town. Soon, they had a thriving business and things finally seemed to be looking up for them.

One day, Washington started crouching over in excruciating pain.

"Charolette, I am not feeling well," he mumbled through his pain. "I think I need to go the doctor."

The doctor's office was about twelve miles away from where they were living. Charolette rushed out of the house to call the neighbor with the one car at that time to assist her with getting Washington to the hospital. The neighbor was willing and able. She came back inside to see Washington twisting and turning in pain. She had never seen him like this before so Charolette became extremely distraught over the whole thing. Her heart was just racing and all kinds of thoughts were just going through her mind.

They eventually set out. When they got to the hospital, Washington was rushed into the Emergency Room and they ran some tests on him. They found out he had a stomach virus. Charolette was not sure what he had eaten or how this had come about. The doctors told them he would have to stay the night for further observation. Charolette stayed with Washington the night by his bedside within the hospital room. It wasn't much, but she made herself comfortable watching him sleep. The next morning, he arose looking much better than the day before. She asked him how he was feeling and he replied "much better" so that was good sign for her.

He was discharged with strict orders to take the prescribed medication which was some antibiotics that would clear up the virus and to drink a lot of fluid for the next two days. So they went on home. Charolette told Washington to just get some bed rest because, since they had returned from the city, he had been just working extremely hard planting and harvesting the crops from the farm.

Getting him to stay in bed was a challenge by itself Washington was never a lazy man. Like her father, he tried to make the best of his day. After a day, he was up and about wanting to return to his regular daily schedule of turning the soil and catering to the few cattle they had in the fields. Charolette was strongly opposed to him being back in the fields so soon.

"Charolette," he said in his simple, sweet voice, "stop worrying yourself. I'll be alright."

"Washington, you need to adhere to the doctor's instruction and rest for the two days. The farm not going nowhere."

She convinced Washington to stay in bed for another day as per the instruction from the physician at the hospital. She took care of him for those two days with everything she had to give. He was so appreciative.

"Charolette," he said, "I thank God for you. You're a beautiful woman with a heart of gold and committed to your family. I couldn't have asked for more in this life and if I have to do it all over again there is absolutely no one in this world that I would rather spend my life with but you."

The tears filled his eyes. There was a sense of sincerity and passion about that statement. Charolette's heart was bursting with love and compassion for this wonderful man. So she hugged him tightly and whispered in his ears:

"I've always loved you more than you'll ever know. We were meant to be together and nothing in this world can separate us. Neither death or whatever else come our way in this life."

They went to bed feeling blessed and just a feeling of renewed commitment. Their marriage was on a firm foundation and nothing would cause it to crumble.

The next day, they woke to a new day, vibrant and energized by the beauty of the morning sun. Washington returned to his regular scheduled daily function of tending to the farm and Charolette was home taking care of the house. She had also started to assist with some of the folks who at the time were having difficulties reading and writing their loved ones. The postmistress side of her was still very much alive.

On one dreary evening, Washington came in from the farm complaining about a different problem. His chest was tightening up on him and at one point, he could not breathe.

"Well, that is it. You will not go the farm tomorrow," Charolette said. "We'll have to go the city at the island's major hospital to get this checked out. Tightening of chest is never a good sign for anyone."

Charolette wasn't ready to lose the love of her life while there were alternatives in terms of medical care. She was adamant in getting him the care and medical attention he needed at any cost; so they packed their bags to catch the early bus that passed the house 5:30 am each morning for the city. On their way, there were a lot of things going through her mind *Why, God, at this time? I'm not ready to lose him. I don't know how I will make it without him.*

Washington never really said much. He never really spoke unless it was necessary and probably he had been feeling those pains for a long time and just didn't want to say it, feeling he did not want to put excess pressure on his wife.

They arrived at the hospital on time and went in to the triage area of the Emergency Room. Charolette explained to the nurse the symptoms Washington was having and she did necessary tests. The surgeon also came and did the basic evaluation of Washington and found nothing wrong with him that would warrant hospitalization.

"Charolette, I told you nothing wasn't wrong. I don't know why you always worrying yourself over nothing and get excited as soon as I say I am having a little pain."

"Well, Washington, if you are not going to take your health serious I will."

Charolette was little perturbed hearing him saying that. It was not as if she had gone to the hospital for herself. She had felt he had a genuine health problem and it was better to know than not to know. She could not afford him falling dead at her feet. He meant too much to her. Losing another good man from her life would only be devastating. She was still left wondering if there was anything more she could have done to save her own father.

The Silent Hurt of Charolette Erica Atwell

"Ok, sweetheart, you are absolutely right. I promise you I'll take my health more serious so don't get mad. I just feel as if sometimes I depend on you too much. When we got married, that was one of our commitments we made to each other. Through sickness and health, we'll be there to comfort and support each other no matter what. We can't live this precious life of ours thinking we can do all things by ourselves and sometimes our selfish behavior causes us more pain and hurt than you can even imagine. Our life should be an example to our children and anyone else we come in contact with to teach them the joy of marriage."

Unfortunately, Washington was never the same after that last visit. He started to become reclusive and was just not the quiet fun loving person he used to be. Charolette was troubled by the way he was looking as each day passed. He assured her nothing was wrong; he was just at a stage in his life where he thinks he needs to slow down because he's been working since the age of ten. About a month after that conversation, one night he called Charolette and was just talking a lot of things that wasn't making much sense to her. He asked for Olivia and Richard.

"Washington, they are living in the city so they can't be here."

"Charolette, tell them how much I love them and they mean the world to me."

"Washington, why are you saying all of this to me? I don't understand at all."

He held her hands tightly and was caressing them with this passion she had never felt before from him. She was just emotionally drained not knowing what was going on.

Washington did not wake up the next morning. He died in his sleep. Charolette broke down. She had been laying beside him all night and did not even know he died. She was in a state of bewilderment. *How could this happen to me? I didn't deserve it not one bit?* Charolette stood there, tears rolling down her cheeks as she called, "Washington, please get up. Please get up. Don't leave like this."

She could hear her own screams getting louder and louder, sounding as if it was someone else. Finally, the neighbors heard and came over to find her one and only true love laying there with this peaceful look on his face dead, Charolette was devastated. Her heart felt like it was ripped out. She was in a place of deep mourning. She sent telegrams to Olivia and Richard informing them of their father's death.

Within a day or two, they were there. After that, everything just seemed to become a blur. Her mind wasn't in the right place at that time. The entire neighborhood came by the next morning. Some were there to just observe; others were there to express their condolence and some were there just to be inquisitive. Charolette tried to gather her thought process because at some point she had to get it together. There were a lot of things to be done in terms of informing his relatives and the few friends she knew of.

She stand there and watch as the pain tugged at her heart while the Medical Examiner removed her beloved's body so that they could perform an autopsy and find out the cause of death. That would take a little time anyhow so during that time she was able to make the funeral arrangements for him, her mind still in a deep fog. She could not recall if she had felt this much pain at the deaths of either of her parents.

On the day of the funeral, Charolette was overwhelmed with grief and anger, asking "Why, Lord, did you take him so soon?" She was just a mere shadow of her natural self. George Washington Atwell was buried in the Elliott family plot beside Charolette's other family members, including her father and mother.

After Washington's death, Charolette went into seclusion, staying away from everybody she knew that would want to get close to her. Her children were worried sick for her in terms of her not being able to function as she should. She just could not find the energy to do anything. So she lived her life in a bubble with no regards for life. Even to do the smallest thing became a challenge. She was extremely angry and would snap at the slightest thing.

Now she understood her mother's grief and resulting deep depression when she too lost the love of her life.

Charolette's two eldest children tried to console her but she snapped at them.

"Are you happy now that he died? Because you never really liked him. I can tell you he is the best thing that ever happened to me apart from my parents. I hope you are happy now."

When she realized what she had said to her children, it finally hit her that she was taking out her anger on those who didn't deserve it.

For the next couple of years, Charolette refused to get involved in any relationship because she could not find the courage to do so. She made the conscious effort to keep herself away from doing anything that would hurt Washington. Even in his death, she still had that love and respect for him. She lived her life just the way a married couple should live by honoring his sacrifice and commitment to his family. What more could she have done to cherish such a human being who had been so full of life and purpose driven?

Charolette found ways to occupy herself with other things in the community. She took a more active role in the church, organizing community meetings to discuss the issues and concerns of the people who are less fortunate and didn't have the resources to speak for their rights. Emotionally, she was in denial of Washington's passing as if it wasn't affecting her in any shape or form. She learned to disguise the pain and anguish in a way that was discreetly frightening. She had always been the strong one, but she couldn't handle the pressure of not having him around; the task was just too daunting. She was getting by each day with the bare minimal effort of just providing for herself and doing the things that was necessary to keep her sane.

One night, Charolette had a dream where Washington came to her and said:

"Why are you so worried about me Charolette? I'll be alright. You don't have to worry that much. Where I am its fine. Find a way to live your life to the fullest."

She jumped out of bed with tears flowing down her face not knowing what it was, asking herself "Am I hallucinating or what? This is way too strange for me." She sat up in the bed for a period of time, unable to go back to sleep. Furthermore, she was scared as ever, as if he was there in the flesh. She felt his presence so much it was surreal, to say the least.

When the sun rose in the morning, the glare came through the windowpane and Charolette felt a peace come over her that she'd never felt before. That is when she knew there was something more than just mourning. The passing of a loved one is never an easy process no matter how much we think we are resilient and strong; it can tear the whole fiber of our being to pieces.

Charolette had renewed strength that morning, feeling vibrant and well rested. She had no idea where all of that vitality came from, but she was feeling renewed and hopeful.

On this specific morning, she was able to walk for a mile to just clear her mind and enjoy the beauty of the island. It had been a long while since she had done that. If only Washington was there to enjoy it with her. During the days when she was feeling down and out, she would just recall the great times they had spent together. Those memories satisfied her longings in ways no one could imagine.

Of all the children, Washington's death affected Richard the most. He never cried when his father died. He just sat there in a daze and never said much. Richard never talked about missing his father or even uttered a word about his father's death. Earlier in his life, Richard and his father had had a tumultuous relationship. Richard had started to keep bad company and Washington was adamant that he wouldn't' go down that path; not while he was living. He would make sure he achieved his full potential. Many trips to the city had been made to try to set the boy straight.

The Silent Hurt of Charolette Erica Atwell

Richard was very stubborn and never really listened to anyone but himself, so there was always a clash of will power. At one point, it got real physical between Washington and Richard. It caused a lot hurt and pain on both sides. For a long time, it was difficult and strained relationship between them. Richard was a lot like his father so it was difficult for them to come to some meaningful resolution. Richard had come to the realization that it wasn't a good idea to walk around with this anger towards his father and his energy could be well used in a positive way. So they had started to mend the long standing feud. Washington's death had brought on more pain for Richard. He loved his father in ways it was hard to imagine.

The fact of the matter was that Washington was doing what any father would have done to protect his children from the elements of society. The day Washington and Richard sat on the porch talking and emotions were just flowing was a pivotal point in their relationship. Washington was able to explain to him his upbringing and the difficulties he faced as a child. That conversation solidified the relationship and brought on new meaning of father and son relationship. If that porch could have talked, it could have told many stories of healing that had taken place in that very place.

The Silent Hurt of Charolette Erica Atwell

Emotionally Hurt

Richard migrated to the United States a few weeks after his father's death. This did not sit very well with Charolette. Richard reminded Charolette so much of his father; furthermore, he was her last belly pain. He was everything like his father: didn't talk much, just very observant and only spoke when it was necessary. This was just too much for Charolette; to lose two of the men in her life that she absolutely adored and loved one after the other was a lot for her to bear.

On the day he was leaving, Richard promised his mother that no matter what he'd make sure she would visit the United States someday; at whatever cost, he'd make it happen. About three years passed and nothing happened, even though during that time he was sending a little money for her to sustain herself. Then, one day she received an invitation from Richard. He was getting married and he wanted his mother and sister Olivia to attend the wedding. Charolette's whole thought process changed.

In that instant, she knew she was about to have new experience. She also received a letter in the mail stating that both she and Olivia had interviews at the United States Embassy in the city.

It was a Monday morning. Olivia and Charolette were dressed as if they were going to a ball; you know those clothes you have set aside for special occasions. On reaching the embassy, they could see there were long lines of people waiting, all with the same intentions of migrating to the United States for a better way of life. Life was just too difficult on the island at the moment. People were basically struggling to make the necessary ends meet. As Olivia and her mother stood in the line in an orderly fashion, those who were at the front of the line started to enter. After a while, a lot of people were coming out with tears in their eyes. They had been denied a visa. The fear inside rose to a new level of anxiety. Charolette was wondering if she would get the visa to travel for her son's wedding. Olivia seemed even more nervous than Charolette was.

They were called individually into separate rooms. The Consulate didn't ask Charolette many questions; only the basic ones which were pretty simple. Olivia wasn't that fortunate; she was denied a US visa. She was devastated and crying uncontrollable. Charolette had received a ten year visa and was just too excited to even notice what was going on with Olivia. As they were travelling back home, it dawned on her, "Oh my, Olivia was denied." The guilt Charolette felt at that time was unspeakable. She hugged her daughter and promised her, "Whatever happens, I'll make sure you alright in terms of sending whatever I can send for you."

The plan was put into place for Charolette to travel in the summer month of July that year which was close to the time of the wedding. A part of her was torn knowing Olivia wasn't able to travel with her.

Charolette arrived in the United States with her visa in hand, feeling all jubilant and mostly excited at the prospect of attending her last child's wedding. She was overwhelmed with joy. Richard had come to the airport to get her and she assumed he was waiting outside for her.

The Silent Hurt of Charolette Erica Atwell

When the plane was about to land, looking through the window, all Charolette could see was the beauty of the lights, just awesome and splendid. The place was huge in comparison to the airport on the island. There were a lot of people waiting to remove their luggage from the conveyor belt. Charolette watched as her luggage come around and she leaned over to retrieve it. It was somewhat heavier than she remembered. A kind young man assisted her with lifting the luggage off the conveyor belt. The difficult part for her was to get out from the section where it said 'Arrival'. The place was strange to her and most of all crowded with people going in all directions. It was in some ways similar to arriving in Canada but also very different in the way people moved more quickly.

Charolette stopped for a moment to read the sign on the overhead board where it instructed you to Exit and she just followed the directions. After all, she was not new to traveling. On reaching outside, Richard was there to greet her with open arms. They drove for the next forty-five minutes before they arrived at his house where he was living with his fiancé.

The houses were in close proximity to each other and to huge shopping malls. The space, roads, and buildings amazed Charolette. It seemed so different than Canada and even more so than the island she had just left behind. They entered the modest home and Charolette looked around, somewhat proud of his accomplishments. It was pretty clean and well-kept. Everything was in place. The welcome by his fiancé was even more special; she was extremely warm and welcoming. Richard showed Charolette where she would be staying and they sat there for a long time just talking about how she missed his father and how he would be so proud of her seeing that she did not turn out to be a statistic.

As Charolette talked, she felt the old feelings being stirred up with all the joy and pain that came with them. She found herself getting really emotional. Richard hugged her and reminded her that "God knows best; where he is I am sure he is looking at us and smiling with great pride that you are here." That statement gave her some peace.

"I know," Charolette responded, "you are just like your father, loving kind and compassionate to those who you love. You remind me so much of him. Your features are exactly the same, the way how you walk and talk, it's uncanny."

Charolette went to bed feeling a sense of joy knowing that she was in place where she was comfortable. It brought peace to her innermost being. As the wedding drew closer, Charolette and her son got much closer. His wife-to-be was kind and loving. She had a lot of good qualities about her that Charolette absolutely adored. Furthermore, she was marrying her son and was going to be definitely a part of the family no matter what.

On the day of the wedding, Charolette was well dressed, feeling all beautiful. She hadn't felt this way in a long time. She was going to a celebration of life, love, joy and happiness. She was most happy for her son Richard. She was beaming with pride and sincere hope that their marriage would stand the test of time.

The wedding ceremony was a wonderful proceeding, although the pastor made some mistakes a few times like he must have been drunk or something. Sandra, Charolette's daughter who was living in the United States and whom she hadn't heard from or seen in a long time came to the wedding with her daughter. That was also a major surprise for Charolette.

Charolette was just elated seeing God's handiwork being performed. There had been many nights she had kneeled at her bedside asking God to protect him with his grace and mercy. When Richard was in his teens, he had a very bad temper that would sometimes raise its ugly head. Charolette was always troubled by it. The company he was keeping also was not good. The path he was heading down was a place of desolation and turmoil, so her only weapon at that time was to call on the name of Jesus. So, to see him grown to be the man he had become was just the work of many nights of prayer over his life. She loved this child with all she had. He reminded her so much of his father.

After the wedding ceremony at the church, the reception was held in a different part of the city about one hour away from where the church was. The guests were all dressed up in their suits and ties. His best friend from childhood Derrick was also there. They had given a lot of trouble as teenagers so it was a big family re-union.

They finally arrived at this beautiful hotel where the reception was being held. It was well decorated with beautiful flowers the overall ambiance was to die. The guests were arriving in time while the bride and the groom went to take pictures and enjoy their special day before coming to the reception hall. Charolette recalled her own wedding to Washington. It had not been as spectacular as this one. Theirs had been a simple but unified marriage. Now, she was experiencing a wedding at a larger scale and it was a wonderful feeling.

The Silent Hurt of Charolette Erica Atwell

Charolette's heart ached. She wished Washington was there to experience the moment, watching their son going through what would, perhaps, be the best day of his life. It was so magical as the bride seemed to float in her white dress. Although she had found the strength to go on, it still sometimes sat on her like an elephant and she often felt like she was drowning, suffocating in the pain. It tore through her sometimes she felt weak. But she was learning to move forward and take one step at a time.

The wedding reception was going on but Charolette realized that she was not happy with what she was hearing. People were coming up to make a toast to the bride and groom. She was in a state of disbelief at the rhetoric that was coming out of their mouths. It was an abomination unto union. Right there and then she felt a sense of pity for her child. Never in her life had she heard such reprehensible and disgusting things being said at a wedding. When it was her time to speak, Charolette stood proudly and addressed her son and his wife:

"From the first time I met you, I loved you as a daughter. You are a beautiful girl with a lot love and kindness. I wish you well. I wish you health. I wish you God's love and prosperity and I love you both."

With all the nonsense that was being said before, it was refreshing to hear something that really made sense. What kind of human being would come to a wedding ceremony and act like that in saying things that were inappropriate to a newly married, decent couple? In that very moment, Charolette was overcome with hurt and disappointment, feeling that her child was in a bad situation, not so much with his wife, but the family that he was getting into. They were not displaying the class that Charolette was used to.

The Silent Hurt of Charolette Erica Atwell

She was extremely hurt during the whole reception phase. However, she hugged him and reminded him of the goodness of his father and what he stood for.

While she was in the United States, Charolette decided she should visit her son Jacob who was living in Colorado with his wife and children.

She was greeted with open arms by her eldest son whom she had not seen in about fifteen years. She had been longing to see him. A part of her felt like she was on this final leg of her journey because of how things were just unfolding rapidly. Jacob was doing quite well for himself. He wasn't in any kind of desperation or financial ruin. She was happy to see his wife whom she had known from she was just a young girl.

The house that he was living was very spacious. They had four children but the love for family was quite evident. Charolette was feeling very much at home; not many from the island had the opportunity to experience this kind of blessings. Charolette's mind took her back to one occasion when she was walking to the store back home on the island and a relative saw her and they stopped and began to talk about just about everything. All of a sudden, the conversation changed in a way that caught Charolette off guard. "Charolette, look how many of your children are living abroad and none of them can help you to get out of this God forbidden place."

"What is that to you?" Charolette replied, "And why you would even have the audacity to ask such questions?"

Richard was just a teen then and was spending time with Charolette in the country for his summer holiday Charolette returned home in tears and he asked, "What

The Silent Hurt of Charolette Erica Atwell

wrong with you, mommy?" and she told him what her first cousin by her mother's side had said to her.

"One day I'll be able to help you see the beauty of the United States," he promised in that moment.

To see that she was there travelling to different states and cities because of his promise was a blessing for Charolette.

So, she spent about year with Jacob in Colorado. Unfortunately, the weather was getting to her. The cold was just too great for her to handle and wearing a thick coat for so long was proving too much. She wanted to see the sunshine of her homeland.

Charolette was getting a little home sick. She was longing for home, to go back and make sure Washington's burial site was clean and free of debris. She had stayed in Colorado long enough; it was time to go back New York and see Richard and his family. That was her final stop before she headed back home to the island.

She spoke to him prior to returning to New York City. When she came back, the joy she had felt before was gone. Richard and his wife had a beautiful baby girl who just adorable. Both Richard and his wife were working at the time. They rose early in the morning and came back home around six in the evening. Charolette found out it was going to be difficult for her to be staying home by herself.

One morning, Charolette wanted a cup of tea so she went into the kitchen and tried to turn the stove on to heat the water. All she heard was this clicking sound. She did not know where it was coming from. Richard was standing there looking at her with a sad look on his face.

The Silent Hurt of Charolette Erica Atwell

"Mother," he finally said, "you can't stay here by yourself. It is too risky. Just standing there watching you trying to light the stove was really an eye opening experience. You could have burned down the house or even more serious burn up yourself. So what I'll do, I am going to talk with Sandra to keep you during the week and I will come for you on Friday evenings to spend the weekend."

Charolette was left alone for that morning with instruction not to try and turn on the stove but just wait until either of them got home. Richard made sure he set everything aside that morning, even though he knew he would get to work late. But that didn't matter one bit. When Richard got home, Charolette got her things together because she was looking forward to spending some time with her daughter in the other borough.

When they got there, it wasn't as pleasant as Charolette thought it would be. The reception she received was cold and bitter.

"She can't stay because we don't have the space to accommodate her," Sandra declared. "Furthermore, you are her son so you need to keep her."

As if she wasn't her daughter. Charolette was standing there for a while before she could even respond to such insensitive remarks and disrespect to her own mother. She looked at Richard as if for an answer.

The Silent Hurt of Charolette Erica Atwell

Charolette Rejected

When I tried to explain to my sister the reasons for me taking mother to see her, the argument got way out of control. Some mean words were expressed right there and then. Charolette did not say anything about what was occurring, but I could see the hurt through her tired eyes. I was literally pleading with her eldest daughter to take her just for the weekends and I'd definitely come and get her on Friday evenings. After much resistance, it was agreed on that I'd come back for her on Fridays. Before I left my sister's place that evening, a major part of me was torn as I realized what was going on with this wonderful person who had dedicated her life to her family and children. I went over to hug her. The coldness I felt was like I was in a subzero freezer; right there and then my entire body felt like it was in a tail spin.

So I walked for a minute with tears in my eyes knowing the pain we'd just caused one of the greatest human beings alive. I know we have our lives to live, but this one situation was far too hurtful for me to accept the mere fact that Charolette was being bounced around and feeling as if she was not welcome in her children's home.

Charolette was devastated in more ways than one; she was feeling un-loved from all sides. It bothered her to the point where she wanted to go back to the island because in her mind she was more comfortable and at peace there. Then there was this big family feud that erupted. There were family members calling from all over God's green earth pointing fingers at each other and blaming who did what from who should have done what. It was very ugly.

The Silent Hurt of Charolette Erica Atwell

Charolette had gotten caught up in all of the nonsense because everyone was trying to get her on their side to blame one another. Charolette wasn't that kind of person anyhow; not a bone in her body was like that. She could be a little abrupt at times and even a little manipulative to get her point across. Other than that, she was the sweetest person you'd ever want to meet.

I remember one night I was home and the house phone rang. It was my brother Jacob on the other line. Right off the bat, he was just attacking me with some choice words. I listened to all of his colorful words for a while. Even when it was time for me to respond, he was just rambling on about everything from life to my upbringing as a child to my current situation with my wife. It was really bad but I listened some more. Then I got to the point where I said, "Enough is enough" and responded in a colorful way too.

The surprising thing during that conversation is that some deep-rooted anger and hate came up that I didn't even know as a child my dad Washington had to bear. The nastiness that was coming out of Jacob's mouth was unbearable and disgusting to me. Since that day, some of us have not spoken to each other. It was a moment in life where you wanted to dig a hole and go inside to hide from all the hurt.

Charolette was in more pain than before. In one of our conversations, she said to me:

"Son, I love you more than life itself. I can't understand why they are making a big fuss over this situation regarding you. You did what was necessary at the time to protect me and most importantly your family. Furthermore, I don't know why all of a sudden everybody

The Silent Hurt of Charolette Erica Atwell

showing interest. Where were they when I was back in the island struggling to make ends meet? You and I have traveled all over the island selling every little thing we could put our hands on to provide food and shelter. At this point in my life I am very comfortable with what I've done for my children. I have absolutely no regrets or the desire to continue with being passed around to each of you where there is so much contempt and bickering. My heart is overwhelmed with hurt. I want to tell you especially thanks for your kindness in allowing me to visit the United States, because you know what it was. You who saw the desire to get me here and I am forever grateful. I don't even know why the rest of them making a big fuss over nothing. They have been here longer than you have been. Never one time had any of them ever offered me help in getting here. Within two years you had lived up to your promise you had made to me in providing for me in the best way possible. That was a touching moment for me, son. I don't love you more than any other of my children but the bond I have with you, I never really had that with any of the other children. I'm not sure if it is because you remind me so much of your father Washington. You have the same demeanor. You are extremely kind and love your family in ways that they wouldn't understand even if you wrote it in big bold letters. Each of you has a different personality, which is a trait that is unique to each of your abilities.

You have grown to be such a wonderful man. Keep your priorities in life that are essential for you to excel at whatever your heart desires. Focus on being a person of character rather than just living your life to please everyone, because at the end of the day, you'll find out the

The Silent Hurt of Charolette Erica Atwell

importance of life is what you've done in good faith that really matters. I am at a stage in life now where my will power is declining to the point I feel I can't continue staying here with you. All the urge for me to go back home is far too great. All those many a nights you sat up with me sewing bags and chatting while everyone was asleep, you don't know how much it meant to me.

Your sister Olivia is so much like me. She cares for her family and will give them the clothes off her back without even thinking she'll go naked. Olivia is much more like me: beautiful spirit of love and genuine concern. She can even be a little manipulative when she wants to. I wonder where she got that from?. Don't ever forget her. In whatever you do, hold on to her with all you've got."

The conversation ended with:

"Son, I am so tired of this cold and madness. Everybody seems to be in a hurry. I want to go back home to the beautiful scenery of the island and live out my days."

I was taken aback by that last statement. It was as if she knew something that we didn't know, or was setting us up to knowing of any kind of illness that was taking its toll on her. Charolette was never one to complain about any and everything; she wouldn't even mention it if she was feeling severe pain. She bottled up every hurt and desire inside her.

The Silent Hurt of Charolette Erica Atwell

Returning Home

When it was time for Charolette to return home to the island, she was saddened about being in the United States and the way she was treated. Charolette's stay was an eventful one, to say the least.

Charolette had started to get things prepared for her return. She was buying every little thing she could get her hands on to take home. For the rest of her time, Charolette was just going through the motion of biding her time, anxiously awaiting the date to return home. The flight was booked for her return home to the island.

About a week prior to her scheduled trip, Charolette was able to build up the courage to tell everyone how she felt about staying in the US with her children. It wasn't all a pleasant experience so it was something deep down inside her that she was able to suppress and hide in a way, harboring the silent hurt she felt. In one of her conversations with her daughter-in-law, she made it quite clear how the whole thing affected her. Knowing after all she had done for her children out of the little she had, it was absolutely disappointing and painful. Charolette had become extremely silent and withdrawn; she wasn't speaking much about anything. The conversation had re-ignited about how she was treated. The unfortunate thing was that most of who was making assumption and criticizing wasn't much better either.

The day was almost here for Charolette to leave the United States. Most of the things she had gathered to take with her were for relatives and friends. Charolette was very frugal with her spending, but she was kind to those who were in need and would give her last to help someone. She had

The Silent Hurt of Charolette Erica Atwell

always been a proud woman in many ways like her mother. What she had hoped for staying with her sons and daughter-in-law was that all the sacrifice she had made would somehow resonate with them to treat her with unconditional love.

Charolette had made arrangement for her grandkids to pick her up from the small airport on the island. The day she had called and spoke to the kids about returning home they were excited. Charolette murmured to herself, "at least someone cares to see me." Her daughter in-law overheard the remarks and wasn't happy about it. Charolette was confronted in an aggressive manner and was promptly told of her manipulating behavior and being passive aggressive and most of all she didn't fight or argue fair. Well that set off a whole new round of arguments where old wounds were reopened. It wasn't pretty.

You see, Charolette had bottled up everything inside for a long time; furthermore, she wasn't the one who let go of anything that easy. The tone of the conversation or cursing was just too toxic and painful. Things were said that shouldn't have been said; hurtful things that had been laying dormant and started to raise its ugly head. Charolette was able to express her true feelings about the whole situation; it was brutal, to say the least.

Her daughter in-law was fuming mad, also in a rage of total disbelief, asking how someone could be so ungrateful and insensitive to those who tried to help them. The argument carried on for a while until I stepped in to squash the argument between them. The problem with that was that I was getting ultimatums from both sides. I wasn't going to be drawn into such a battle because, at the end of the day the wife and mother play different roles in my life

The Silent Hurt of Charolette Erica Atwell

and I certainly would not allow myself to make any rash decision.

I tried to be neutral, not taking any side and became the target of accusations in terms of whose side I was always on. Then, I tried to explain again.

"This is not resolving anything. You both are acting out of character. That is not how adults should behave. We are in the house with children and the both of you got so caught up in what is just utterly disgusting and senseless conversation that is just causing more hurt rather than a solution."

After that last confrontation, much wasn't said. Actually, they ignored and avoided each other in every possible way. The tension was so great you could sense it a mile away. Charolette knew her time was drawing near to return home to her beloved homeland. She was looking forward to that more than anything else.

One evening while the family was out dinner, we all sat around this huge table. Everyone was sharing their favorite moment on what they are thankful for. Most of the family members were thankful for having family around who cared and loved each other. Charolette was silent and wasn't saying anything about what was being said around the table. I reached over to her and gently asked her:

"Why are you so quiet?"

In her usual sarcastic tone she replied:

"I can't be around hypocrites. Listening to the nonsense when you and I know the real truth."

The Silent Hurt of Charolette Erica Atwell

It was kind of discouraging hearing her response. My heart was overwhelmed with sadness and a sense of disappointment.

"Mother, what is wrong with you? Why can't you learn to let go of things that won't add any value to anyone including yourself?"

She looked at me with this unusual grin on her face and quickly put me in my place, reminding me of her role in my life and how she raised me not to allow any woman to rule and control every single aspect of my life. I was in awe and confused at the same time. I couldn't even respond to what I'd just heard.

The whole table where we were sitting having dinner mouth drop; it was like some of them had seen a ghost. At that moment, she started to point out every single thing that ever happened while she was staying with the family. Charolette went on for about five minutes sharing her opposition to things that got her real upset. In my state of shock and awe, some of the things she was saying made a whole lot of sense and kind of gave me a sense of guilt.

On the other hand, my significant other wasn't happy at all. The expression on her face was like she would want to get up and turn everything over. I looked over at her and whispered in her ears, "let me deal with this." After Charolette had finished with her rant, I gently reminded her how inappropriate her behavior was and hurtful in terms of her knowing full well she had all these issues inside her and allowed it to fester to the point where it felt like anger. The children were asking her:

"Grandma, what happened?"

The Silent Hurt of Charolette Erica Atwell

Charolette's outburst in front of the kids troubled me the most. I really don't think it was necessary in an environment such as this. I was hoping it would be a celebratory mood after spending so much time with us , so I guess all along when she was saying she missed home it was more a feeling of resentment and rejection.

There wasn't anything that Charolette had inside her boiling up like hot water she hadn't expressed her feelings about. A part of me was hurting and felt as if I had let my mother down and disappointed her to the point of watching her breaking down. The tears from Charolette's eyes were flowing down her slender face. I leaned over and rubbed my hand through her long, beautiful, now silver hair. Her whole body was shaking. That was when I realized that sometimes people can be hurting in such a way and hide their feelings because of the fear of not knowing how one will respond. In this situation, Charlotte wasn't just anyone; she was my mother.

How could I have allowed this to happen and was so blind in not knowing my mother that I've loved dearly and adore get to the point of such internal pain? When I remembered all the sacrifice she had made for her children and seeing her at this juncture in her life, it was heart wrenching. I was extremely glad that what had occurred in that restaurant gave me insight into my mother and who she was.

After we left the restaurant, there was a deafening silence in the car. No one was saying anything at all; everyone was just staring in space as if they were in an abyss. Charolette was also in a mood of dejection and it seemed as if the weight of the world was off her shoulders. At that moment, I realized her perspective on what her true feelings were.

When we got home, I was still feeling the effect of the conversation in the restaurant so I decided to continue talking with my mom. I asked her if she would mind if we continued the conversation from where we left off and she said no, she would love to, because there are things that she would like to tell me in person. When she said that, my ears pricked up. I asked myself what this could be after all that had happened just couple hours ago. What else could there be to talk about?

So we went outside on the patio. While we were there just going over what had happened at the restaurant, there were a lot of things that came to mind. Some of her concerns were valid and needed to be addressed right away. Sometimes we can get so caught up in the daily process of life that we tend to forget what matters most. Charolette was making a lot sense in terms of her expressing her feelings and emotional instability. I sat there listening and absorbing Charlotte's long standing internal issues.

My wife came out and said to her:

"I'm not here to intrude on your conversation with your son, but what happened at the restaurant I just couldn't sit knowing fully well my heart and conscience was not clear. So, I need to let you know the internal wound you caused me, and it's bothering me to the core of my heart. I don't think I am a bad person. We all have our shortcomings and faults and bad behavior."

Charolette responded by letting her know how she was a selfish and controlling individual who showed a lot

The Silent Hurt of Charolette Erica Atwell

passive aggressive behavior. Well that didn't go well. The argument escalated to a different level. I stepped in between them trying to calm both of them down. It was just pure screaming and hollering. It got to the point where there was just a whole lot of name calling. I actually was disappointed in both of them.

After a while, enough was enough. I raised my voice to a level I'd never done before. They looked at me with shock and immediately stopped the bickering.

"Let's resolve this issue as adults and not like we're fighting in the streets," I bellowed, trying to get control of my own voice.

Charolette was remorseful and started to apologize in ways I had never seen her do before. Knowing her, that was unusual. She broke down in tears, crying uncontrollably and her body was shaking. I put my arms around her, rubbing her shoulders in an effort to console her, reminding her that everything was going to be alright. Her daughter-in-law was standing with her mouth open wide in total amazement. I had never seen that look on her face during the years of our marriage.

"Charolette, you're one conniving and evil individual who manipulates your son and everyone you ever come in contact with," my wife accused. "When are you going to stop playing the victim when you very well know your intentions are not good?"

Charolette did not take that description of herself very well. She was about to get real ugly. The gloves were off.

"I am asking you not to do what you're about to do," I pleaded.

The Silent Hurt of Charolette Erica Atwell

"That is what I am telling you about her," Charolette said. "She doesn't have any manners or respect for me. You are my son and part of a mother's responsibility is to protect her children from people who are not genuine and deceitful. I knew this was a bad idea from day one. Even at the wedding her family wasn't happy about the relationship. They thought they are better than you are. I am telling you it was so obvious and clear the blind could have seen the animosity towards you. From that day forward, I realize you are going to be in the fight of your life. Your father and I married for all those years, God rest his soul, and I never spoke to him in the manner she speaks to you. That is what bothers me about her so I won't sit here thinking that all is well with you. I would be a fool."

That description from Charolette stirred up a new argument because her daughter-in-law felt as if she was being disingenuous and sarcastic towards her and her family. So, here I was, caught between a rock and a hard place, not wanting it to seem like I was taking sides. I am more inclined to defuse the situation. On one hand, my wife was pissing mad at me; on the other, Charolette felt as if I was too weak and couldn't defend myself from the elements of her family who constantly made these remarks and acted as if I was invisible.

My heart was just torn and filled with emotions. A part of me felt Charolette was absolutely right, while the other part of me knew fully well I have the obligation to my wife to support and care for her. Charolette was making a lot of sense in some of the things she was saying. I did not realize how toxic the whole thing had become. For a long time I was in denial and suppressing all of the things that was quite obvious and hurtful to a healthy relationship. I knew right there and then we had a lot to talk about and some serious resolution to make.

When Charolette finished saying her piece, you could see the load was lifted off her shoulders.

"Son, I know I've said a lot and there is a strong possibility that my daughter-in-law will never speak to me again. I am at peace with myself. It is not like I don't love her; I honestly do. But her behavior and her family are just too much for you. Promise you'll sit down with her and talk it over, just the both of you."

I knew right there and then that there were a lot of things to discuss to fix whatever was broken and find out what needed to be done to at least come to some kind of consensus to remove the elephant in the room. Charolette went off to her room to finish packing her suitcase because she was leaving in the morning and returning home to her beautiful island.

Charolette had dreamt of returning home for a long time. Many a night she would sit around the dinner table and reminisce about being home and how much she missed her home. Most of all, she missed her husband and worried daily about his tomb if shrubs had grown and no one would take the initiative to go and cut away the bushes. After all these years, Charolette had this undying love and care for her husband; it was unheard of.

The flight was leaving early in the morning so I took the day off from work to take Charolette to the airport. In-terms of the travelling distance from our house, we were looking at about thirteen miles. On the morning when Charolette was about to leave, she got up real early and

The Silent Hurt of Charolette Erica Atwell

went to the kids' room to hug each of them and tell them how much she loved and cared for them and that nothing in the world meant more to her than her grandkids. Charolette knocked on the bedroom door to tell her daughter-in-law that she was leaving and to thank her for allowing her to spend time in her home.

How can this be when last night Charolette had been in a real bad mood, chiding her daughter-in-law about everything and this morning acted as if nothing had happened? The response was quick.

"Okay, safe travel and take care of yourself. Hope to see you soon."

Charolette reached over at her bedside and hugged her tight and tears started to flow down her face.

"Nothing I said to you last night was personal. But you have to learn how to live your life and cherish what God has given you. Not like I am being bias, but there is too much outside interference and at some point you have to draw the line and care for your family. Will call you when I get home."

We got in the car at approximately 6:45 am and headed for the airport. Charolette and I were able to talk a little about what had occurred over the last couple of days and how it affected her.

"Son, it is your responsibility to do what is right for your family. Make all the necessary effort to cherish your marriage, love your family. Find the time for just you and your wife. Stop being so gullible thinking everything was just going to fall into place like that without hard work and communication."

The Silent Hurt of Charolette Erica Atwell

When we arrived at the airport, I helped Charolette with the bags. There were quite a few suitcases. I guess she was carrying stuff for almost everyone in her community. I had never even bothered to ask. Because if I did, I would get one of those counselling sessions about taking care of those who don't have, cause it was never about any of us ,but what we do for God. Charolette reminded me of how I was raised and what my responsibilities to my family were.

I hugged her as if there were no tomorrow, feeling this sense of heartbrokenness and emotional emptiness. I was just an emotional wreck standing there watching Charolette walk away with her slender frame and long silver hair flowing down her back. I watched for quite a while until I couldn't see her any more. I sat in the airport for two hours, even after her flight had taken off. There was something inside of me screaming and hollering for Charolette who was my rock and confidante.

That was a sad day. I never knew I would miss her so much. The pain was severe in my stomach. The thought of her going back home to live on her own was heart wrenching and came with a lot reservation. Later on that day, Charolette called to let us know she was home safely and enjoying her homeland. Right away, she started to brag about the scenery and the cool breeze and the warmth of the people. I told her I love her and missed her deeply, and I'll come and see her soon. She asked to speak with Grace and I replied, "What?"

"I would like to speak with Grace," she repeated.

That was the first time I heard her mention my wife by name so I was flabbergasted and confused. They spoke for a long time. I did not stand there to listen to the

The Silent Hurt of Charolette Erica Atwell

conversation, but I was filled with joy and a sense of satisfaction. That chapter could be closed now; at least they were at a point where the conversation was civil.

After they finished talking, Grace's face was beaming with a smile, and was at peace. I did not ask her what the conversation was about. I think whatever was said was between the two of them and probably should stay that way. We never heard from Charolette for a long time. I guess she was just re-acquainting herself with being back home and enjoying everything she had missed out on.

One evening, on returning home from work, I went outside to check the mailbox. There was this letter from Charolette. I was so excited to open and read it.

The Letter

Dear Son,

Good day. Greetings in the precious name of Jesus our soon coming king. I am so happy for you and the family. My heart is filled with joy. I am content with myself. Thank you for the birthday card and the Mother's Day gift you sent for me. It couldn't have come at a better time. It was so nice. I adore you and love you with all of my heart.

Well son, I cannot tell you how much I missed you every day and night. I leave you at the throne of God where he will answer prayers. I am praying for you that God will ever keep you under his almighty arms. Bless be to God he is helping you. Dear son, I love you. When I consider you are so far away from me sometimes I sit down and cry. Give my warmest love to Grace. Tell her I love her and I am asking her to take care of herself and also you. God will ever bless her now and always. Since I leave and returned back to the island, things have become extremely difficult in finding the basic necessity. We all have to look to Jesus for he is near at hand. Turn your heart to him. As you know I am old now and the wages is very small. Whatever I received on a monthly basis, it cannot do much. Please, I am asking you for a Bible. The one that I have is old and falling apart. I want the big print. Please read Psalm 36 night and day. I am longing to see you and Grace. May God bless you now and always.

Love and Kisses,

Charolette

When I had finished reading the letter, the tears were just flowing down my face. Because of the sincerity of the letter, I was in awe. Charolette was in state of loneliness and abandonment. That night, I shared the letter with Grace. She also got a little choked up. Charolette was a pure soul, always kind and loving to everyone she came in contact with. Now that she was in the latter part of her years, I was hoping her life would be filled with good things and not worrying about the simple things in life. Charolette had committed all her life to the betterment of her family and was at a point in her life when she needed her family the most. Grace and I sat down and started to strategize how we were going to move forward in making sure Charolette lived comfortably.

The Silent Hurt of Charolette Erica Atwell

Serious Illness

I remember one evening I called Charolette just to see how she was doing. When she got on the phone, she was sounding upbeat and jovial; but there was something inside of me telling me Charolette wasn't okay. So I asked her:

"Are you really ok?"

"Yes, my son, I am doing just fine. Just feeling a little bit of pain here and there."

"Did you go to the doctor?" I asked.

"No," she responded.

Not good; furthermore, the hospital was a long distance off and there were no doctor's office in close proximity for her to go and check out whatever was hurting her. Right there and then I hung up the phone and went to send money through remittance for her to see the doctor the next day. All night I was worried sick about Charlotte's health. My mind was just running wild with all kinds of thoughts and doubts.

Charolette had been a strong and courageous woman for a long time. As far back I can remember, she was the one who was always finding a way to assist someone in need. Definitely, I wasn't going to have a nervous breakdown; but I was so concerned about her health. It was our responsibility to hold her up if she was is in a state of need. Later on that evening, she called the house to let us know that the doctor said she was fine; she just needed to take some bed rest and stay off her feet for a while. Charlotte and Grace spent a long time on the phone just talking to each other which did my heart justice and it gave me a great sense of satisfaction knowing that both of them were at a crossroad and realizing the importance of family.

I was standing in kitchen making a cup of tea when I heard a loud outburst from Grace. I ran inside to see if she was okay. To my surprise, Charolette and Grace were still on the phone sharing stories. Grace said to me:

"Your mother is funny. Talking about since she been back how everyone thinks she brought back the entire United States with her. Everyone was coming making demands what they want."

That was a touching moment for me. After that night, Charolette was inseparable from Grace. They spoke at least two times per week. Over the years, Charolette was never the one who wanted to go the doctor for her regular checkup. Her concept of checkup is boiling bushes for every ailment under the sun. I never understood the significance of that. Norms and culture can sometimes block the importance of health initiatives. At what stage in her journey will she realize that not all bushes can cure ailments? Grace and I sat down and decided that for Charolette to get the best care we need to have someone who could take care of her in real time.

Olivia was living on the island with her husband and kids. The problem with that: she was living at the far end of the island and transportation was scarce and difficult to get around. The next option was to reach out to her and ask her if it would be possible for her to move closer to Charolette and be there to assist her. The conversation did not go well.

A lot of old wounds were reopened and long standing hurts and pain raised their ugly heads. Now it became my responsibility to convince Olivia that it would be just fine for her to move closer to her mother and be her caregiver. She was adamant about not wanting to do it. First and foremost, she was worried about her family and how they would take it, whether good or bad. I assured her it would be just fine; all she had to do was have an open mind about the whole thing. So, we left it at that. The last thing I told her was to sleep on it and talk to her family and I'd get back to her within two weeks.

At that point, the conversation took a turn for good. She seemed more inclined to take on this new phase of her life. Less than two weeks later, I received a call from Olivia stating she would definitely take on the challenge. Setting everything aside from the past, she would welcome the opportunity of taking care of Charolette. We talked about the details and what we wanted to get done which was the taking care of basic needs for Charolette for her to have good life.

I spoke to Charolette and told her about my plan to have someone come and stay with her to assist and help her out. This did not go well.

"Who tell you that I need someone to take care of me?" she asked in her usual sarcastic tone.

"Charolette," I protested, "it is not just anyone; she is your daughter and I asked her to come and take care of you. Right now there is no one that I can think of who will give you the care and the attention that you need more than her."

Charolette went off and reminded me of the relationship they had over the years and I must admit it was never a good one. God knew it took a lot to deal with Charolette in any shape or form. The whole time I was trying to convince Charolette of the positive rather the negative. For years, she and her daughter did not have a good relationship; there was always some kind of clash of personality. I really do believe what caused the problem was that they both had this combative spirit about them so it was easy for her daughter to act and respond in a harsh and sometimes rude manner.

Charolette was blowing smoke all that time, but a part me felt she was open to her daughter coming to help her. The rhetoric was eventually toned down considerably on both sides and, most of all, we were on one page for one common goal. This was a step in the right direction. I knew Charolette loved her independence; but there comes a time in life when we need that help and right at that moment Charolette needed that intervention.

For the next three years, the relationship between Charolette and Olivia grew from strength to strength; that long-standing feud between them subsided dramatically. Both of them were able to put their differences aside and complement each other. Charolette was well taken care of; nothing was spared or anything that her daughter wouldn't do for the love was unwavering and sincere. Charolette was able to do things she had wanted do for a long time after returning home. Now they could go for long walks on the beach and enjoy all the amenities of her beautiful island. Charolette was a big proponent of making the most of the long history of the island and all its beautiful scenery. Funny enough, her daughter had never seen the island in such beauty because she was confined to the far end where there wasn't much to see and do but mountains and mostly farming.

The Silent Hurt of Charolette Erica Atwell

The trust between them grew stronger each day. Charolette was able to pursue some of her passions like volunteering for the basic school about half mile away from her home. Charolette loved children and was compassionate about the well-being of children. Ever since I was a child, Charolette would have numerous kids at any time playing in the yard without a single complaint to their parents. She wasn't this strong disciplinarian, but believed every child should be allowed to flourish and find their true purpose and not stifle the growth of a child. That was her stance on raising children.

Charolette enjoyed the attention she received from the children and a part of me felt she was trying to live her life all over again through the souls of the children around her. Many of the parents were appreciative that Charolette was such a kindhearted person and knowing their children were in a safe environment.

In the latter part of the year, I received a call from Olivia stating that Charolette wasn't doing well and she was concerned about some of things that Charolette was doing. My question to my sister was:

"What would cause you to come to that conclusion?"

"Well brother, she seems to be forgetting things easily and even when I try to remind her it will take a long time for her to even comprehend what I am trying to say or do."

"You know, sis, it is quite natural for someone her age to be going through this phase of life. I don't think it is anything that great you should be worrying about."

"During the nights when Charolette goes to sleep, she talks in her sleep and I promise you, some of the things she is saying is frightening and somewhat troubling."

The Silent Hurt of Charolette Erica Atwell

"What do you overhear that could be 'troubling'?"

"Charolette talks a lot about her childhood in her sleep. Some of the things I think happened during her early childhood about seeing all the hurt and pain her mother had gone through, but was able to suppress those feelings for a long time. Charolette would be crying in her sleep especially when she is mumbling stuff about our father Washington. She misses dad so much after all these years of his death. I never think Charolette had gotten over his death. She walks around with that pain that took the only man she had ever loved. That long-standing pain tends to come more often than anything else. She even shakes or trembles, if you will, in her sleep. Sometimes cold sweat becomes so severe that her clothes are soaked as if she was standing in the rain. I don't think this is normal by any standard. Hopefully, it is nothing too serious that would jeopardize her health and place her in any critical illness."

We decided the right thing to do was to take her to the doctor for a checkup and see if there was anything that was going on with her immune system. As far I knew from limited clinical experience, this could be a sign of Alzheimer's disease which causes memory loss and comes with a lot of risk factors. So I decided to research on what could cause such vibrant and active individual to reach this stage in her life. Knowing how proud and independent Charolette was, this was the last thing on her mind to become dependent on anyone.

Alzheimer's was a progressive disease that moved through different stages of memory loss until the individual was unable to carry on a conversation.

The Silent Hurt of Charolette Erica Atwell

This was exactly what Charolette was going through. The whole dynamics changed in terms of how we were going to give her the care she deserved. I asked my sister to take Charolette to the doctor just to verify that was exactly what had been going on. I didn't want to make an educated guess, because at the end of the day I was not a doctor, so the professional thing to do was to get the right information from a trained professional.

Early that Tuesday morning, I called her about five forty five, in the morning the time I would normally get up for work , just to make sure everything was going according to plan. Sis was already up struggling with Charolette to get ready; that in itself had to be a difficult challenge. Charolette was strong minded and whenever she decided she would not do something, you can bet your last dollar it won't happen. She was stubborn and could be combative at times. So I asked my sister to put her on the phone. There was something about our relationship that whenever we spoke, it was refreshing and a feeling of love just resonated freely.

"Good morning, mother. How are?"

"Am fine son. I don't' know why your sister want to take me to the doctor when nothing is wrong with me."

"Mom, I asked her to because it is the right thing to do. Remember, you're at a stage in life where it is absolutely necessary for you to visit your doctor on a yearly basis or when it's necessary. Please allow sis to take care of you and dress you. You know you have quite a distance to travel."

Her whole attitude changed even with her resentment not wanting to go. Sis came back on the phone and the first thing she said was:

"Our mother love you far more than you can even imagine. I guess because you are her last child and in her words her 'last belly pain'."

Before we hung up the phone, I reminded my sister just to take her time and try to understand that Charolette was at a crossroad in her life; things she used to do had now become so difficult and could cause frustration.

My mind was unsettled at work all that day; my thoughts were just centered on what the doctor would say. I was hoping for the best, but a part of me was expecting the worst. I arrived home from work that evening and saw Grace sitting at the kitchen table. Her demeanor was kind of uncomfortable; she was normally in jovial mood.

"How was your day, hon?" she asked.

"Wasn't so bad. I actually got some things accomplished today. How was yours?"

"Great. Most of what I set out to do today was done. Your sister called about an hour ago to update on your mother's visit to the doctor today."

My heart did a little flip in my chest.

"How was it?" I asked.

"From what your sister said it wasn't all that great, so I think you need to call her so she can explain to you in more details."

The Silent Hurt of Charolette Erica Atwell

Immediately I went and got the phone hanging on the wall in the kitchen and dialed the number to Charolette's home. My sister answered.

"Hey sis. How are you? What happened today at the doctor?"

The news wasn't all that great in terms of her health and I don't think she was taking it too well. I can't remember seeing Charolette sick with any kind of ailment in all the years I'd known her. During the time she was staying with me, only once do I remember taking her to the doctor for an eye exam.

Charolette was diagnosed with High Blood Pressure and was borderline Diabetic and we have to watch her very carefully. She also have to change her eating habits. That never sit well with her, especially when people were trying to dictate to her, telling her what to do and what she can't do. She was adamant about doing what she wanted to do no matter what the doctor said. She believed it was her life and she was going to enjoy it to the fullest.

Charolette came on the phone and was just grumbling and bickering about the whole thing.

"Please, Charolette, are you even listening to yourself? At least you have an idea what needs to be done and how you should go about it. You need to follow the doctor's instruction and change your eating habits."

In one of those sarcastic tones, she asked:

"So all of you going to gang up on me now?"

"Absolutely not! I am more concerned with your overall health, so it's not about ganging up on you. Take this time

The Silent Hurt of Charolette Erica Atwell

to reflect on what changes you are willing to make to live a long and prosperous life."

That night I think she got it.

"It's about time I take care of myself. After all the years I've been giving to everyone and lost focus on doing what is good for me."

I was shocked at her disclosure. That, I do believe was the moment she realized the importance of what we were trying to convey to her.

Within the next two years, Charolette went back and forth to her doctor and was keeping good health. Charolette was even more proud of herself when she realized the significant changes that had occurred in her eating habits. The Sunday before Christmas, the family and I were out shopping for a Christmas tree. We had almost spent the entire day doing some last minute shopping for the kids and picked up a few things my sister had asked me to get for her. When we arrived home, the light on the answering machine was on and there were six messages.

I figured everyone was just calling to wish us Merry Christmas so I kind of went away and ignored it to make a cup of tea. I sat at the kitchen table to have the cup of tea and decided to finally listen to the messages.

I could hardly hear what the first message was saying; but I knew it was my sister. She was crying hysterically. I set the cup of tea aside on the table and called sis, my heart pounding as I tried not to imagine the worst.

"What's going on?" I asked into the phone. "I just got home and was replaying the messages on the phone and you're crying. What's really going on?"

The Silent Hurt of Charolette Erica Atwell

"Charolette is not feeling well," she explained, her voice sounding near to tears. "When she got up this morning, she could not feel her hand or legs. I am so worried."

Sis explained that she called the neighbor who had a car and asked if he could take Charolette to the hospital. When Charolette got to the hospital, my biggest fear was realized. Charolette had a massive stroke; she could not move her hands, legs, and body, and now she's in the Intensive Care Unit at the hospital. My whole world felt as if it had just came to a complete halt.

How could this happen, when she had done everything required by her doctor to maintain good health? There were a lot questions in my mind that needed answers. The turn of events came suddenly. Charolette was going to the doctor on a regular basis; how could this have happened?

Right at that moment, I started to make plans to go home to the island to see Charolette and find out what really happened. I went online to book the ticket. Most of the flights were all booked out because it was the holiday season. I ended up getting a different date just after the holidays which I didn't mind. As long as I was heading home to see Charolette it was fine. Grace also wanted to be a part of the trip because her background was in nursing. Grace worked at the largest hospital in the State; her tenure was about sixteen years as an Intensive Care Unit nurse. That also eased the stress level because some of the questions that I would like to ask, would be definitely from a clinical standpoint with Grace by my side.

We were all set to travel within the next three weeks. I asked Grace's aunt to watch over the kids for us until we returned. A lot of other family members had started to call

The Silent Hurt of Charolette Erica Atwell

to find out the status and I really couldn't articulate anything specific just based on what I had heard so far from my sister back home. Many of these family members I never heard from or even knew about so I was kind of skeptical about giving out too much information.

Exactly a week before we were to travel, my sister called me again to inform me that Charolette was getting worse and I needed to come as soon as possible because all she did was ask for me, when am I coming. She also informed me that the doctor had mentioned Charolette's situation was only going to deteriorate further. The new concern from the doctors with Charolette was that she was losing her eye sight and there wasn't much they could do to save it. Her Glaucoma had gotten worse; not even surgery could save her, that's how bad it was.

The inevitable happened and Charolette lost her eye sight. Now she was dealing with a stroke and blindness. This was just too much for one person to bear. I was so heartbroken and wondered what could have gone wrong that Charolette was suffering so much. Come to think of it, Charolette had never said a bad word about anyone much less to hurt them. With this new revelation, my goal was to get to Charolette as soon as possible. I was just itching to go.

On the day we arrived on the island it was just a wonderful scenery. The breeze was so cool and comfortable; the warmth of the people was overwhelming and pleasant. Even with all of that, my mind could not settle knowing my purpose was far greater than just coming to enjoy the island. I was eager to get to the woman whom I had loved and adored for all my life and now she needed me more than I could imagine. Everything from

The Silent Hurt of Charolette Erica Atwell

there on in was about getting to Charolette, to hug her and kiss her, and tell her how much I love and care for her in ways she could not fathom.

My sister Olivia was waiting at the airport with her husband to take me home. Since I had left the island, there were a lot of changes and new roads, larger buildings, and structures. It felt like I had landed on a strange island that was not my home. All the way home in the car, not much had been said. There was just a silence in the car, a kind eerie feeling if you will. A part of me wasn't sure if I was physically and mentally sound to see Charolette in such condition.

As soon as we got in the house, Olivia started to cry. You see, she'll cry at the drop of a hat. My responsibility at that time was to console her and give her a word of encouragement. I couldn't imagine how difficult it must have been for her watching Charolette go through this terrible phase of her life. The one thing I love about my sister is that she was committed to taking care of Charolette by any means necessary and nothing in this world, absolutely nothing, would prevent her giving Charolette the best possible care.

Not much had changed about the small village where it all started. My mind flashed back to my childhood growing up within the confines of this beautiful paradise. You could see the house from the bottom of the road; it was built on a hill which is not too high. We walked up that small graveled road up to the house and my childhood memories were just wonderful.

The yard, as we entered, teemed with people; some were other relatives whom I've known and some I was meeting

The Silent Hurt of Charolette Erica Atwell

for the first time. It was bitter-sweet reunion. I was in a hurry just to get to Charolette; my soul was on an emotional roller coaster.

As soon as I stepped in the house, Charolette turned her head slightly to the left. Olivia looked over at me and said: "Charolette hasn't done that since all of this happened to her."

"Who is there with you?" Charolette mumbled to Olivia in her beautiful voice. "Is that you?"

"Yes, mom," Olivia replied.

We all became silent. Tears began to flow from Charolette's eyes and down her slender face.

"Son, is that you?" Charolette asked again.

"Yes, mom," I replied.

At that, I broke down in tears and somewhat a sense of joy. I eventually went and sat at her bedside. The first thing she did as she always does is rub my face gently.

"How are you doing? How is your wife and kids? Give them my love."

I responded to her by letting her know Grace was with me. She called Grace over to her bedside and held her hands tightly.

"How are you, my child?"

Grace was also in tears. Through the years, they had their fair share of disagreements and arguments; but the love and compassion were overwhelming. Charolette was not in a somber mood but giving thanks to God for the trials and tribulations and also reminding me of the goodness of God. Charolette never complained.

The Silent Hurt of Charolette Erica Atwell

I sat at her bedside just clinging to her as if I was a child longing for the love of a mother.

"Son, it has been a long and hard road to travel, but you know what, I've lived my life serving in every way possible that I know. My prayers is that I am able to give thanks in whatever the circumstances may be. I miss your father. If he was here he would be taking care of me. Many a night I cry in my sleep thinking of how he left me so soon. At one point I was angry with everybody around me and ostracizing every single one of you. I have learned to accept what God has done for me. Your father was my entire world. We went through some rough passage, but he never raised his voice at me. He never talked down to me. He never raised his hand at me, even when I was at my worst. He always had a word of encouragement and for that I'm grateful. Richard, love your family to the best of your ability. Make every effort to care while you have the energy and time."

That week, I was able to spend some quality time with her, catering to her every need. I knew we were only staying for two weeks so whatever I needed to get done in terms of her health care I had to do it within a certain time frame. One of the most important things on the agenda was to meet with the doctor who had been treating her illness. I needed to get a better understanding of what really happened and since Grace was with me that was even more a priority.

I had gone to the doctor's office two days prior and he was kind of combative and rude, for whatever reason, I was not sure. My initial thought was I felt as if we were asking questions that had not been asked before. I was trying to get him to understand that I was not questioning his ability

The Silent Hurt of Charolette Erica Atwell

to take care of Charolette, but we do have the right to know all the intricate details. So he asked his Assistant to set up some time for us to come so we could sit and talk without any judgment or accusation about Charolette and the care that she received.

On the day of the appointment, Grace and I showed up. The doctor was waiting for us so we greeted each other cordially and from a professional standpoint a much better understanding of my purpose and his role as her Primary Care Physician. He invited us to sit at his conference table in his office with two of his Residents who were a part of Charolette's care. I spoke candidly about why it was absolutely important for me to have a better understanding of what really occurred why Charolette was at the stage she was currently in. The doctor explained the whole process to me. One of the things he mentioned was that Charolette had been ill for quite some time and for the last year her health had been deteriorating rapidly, causing many health concerns.

When the doctor informed us there are more problems that were going to arise for Charolette because of severity of her Hypertension and Hyperglycemia.

"So doctor, what are you actually saying?" I asked.

"The sad fact is, Charolette's leg has to be amputated in order for her to even have a chance of living," he explained. "I know what I am saying to you right know is not what you might want to hear, but from all the clinical testing we have done, that is her only option right now."

Everything went black at that moment. The only thing I remembered is Grace asking, "Are you ok?" So I got myself together and accepted the fact that this was

The Silent Hurt of Charolette Erica Atwell

inevitable. I sat in the doctor's office more confused than I had ever been.

The doctor tried to assure me that it would be fine and Charolette would benefit from the procedure. Even with all of that assurance, my whole world was falling apart for a woman I think is one of the strongest human beings to ever walk this earth. Grace and I were in a state of shock. We were contemplating how we were going to break the news to Charolette and the rest of the family. I just couldn't imagine one person going through so much pain and suffering.

When we got home, the yard was full of people, both family and friends, and even some individuals who just came to ask for something. I got out of the car and went straight inside. I overheard Grace telling some of the people in yard, "He is not in good mood for the simple fact the news from the doctor wasn't all that good. Please understand. He's dealing with a lot."

I went inside the room and sat at Charolette's bedside just looking at her. She must have sensed my presence.

"Richard, is that you?" she asked in the stillness.

"Yes, mom," I answered, trying to inject a note of cheerfulness into my voice.

"Why are you so worried?" she asked.

"I'm not worried," I replied.

"Yes you are. I can hear your heartbeat. Don't worry about things you don't have any control over, son. Whatever God will in our life it will work out. Tell me what the doctor said. It won't matter to me one bit. I've already made up mind to face the consequences. What can be more serious than what I am going through right now? Sometimes in life, son, we act and carry on as if we hold our future. But, remember, none of us have that power to determine our destiny. I have made peace with myself and everything that I've ever done to hurt or cause discomfort to anyone."

Her words reached deep down into my core.

"Well, mom, the doctor said he'll have to amputate one of your legs in order for you to survive and live out the rest of your normal life."

The tears welled up in her eyes. What came after was amazing in my estimation. Charolette grabbed on to my hand and start to pray, telling God how she had accepted her lot and whatever his will in her life she is ready, willing, and able to accept it.

I had at least four more days before I was scheduled to return home to the United States. I knew there were some things that needed to be put in place which were of great importance. I asked Olivia to come into the room to hear what was going to be done because we all so needed her input in whatever was about to transpire.

The procedure for the amputation of Charolette's leg was scheduled for the last Friday of the month at a different hospital. Olivia was just in a state of denial, asking, "Why, does this have to happen to her?" I tried to console her, but the tears were so many I had to get her out of the room. There was a somber mood with most of who were there, including Charolette's grandkids.

Realizing there was the issue with the family members grieving, the thought came to me to take the initiative and be strong for the family. I sensed it was getting out of hand. I asked everyone to gather around so we could come up with some kind of contingency plan to assist Charolette with her care. In my heart, I knew there was no one in this world who would take care of Charolette without ulterior motives like Olivia; she had been a tower of strength, taking care of Charolette from the day she took ill. For that, I was so grateful and full of confidence that she would take care of her mother with the utmost care.

We talked for a while. Everyone had an opinion, advice, suggestion, and comments. No stone was left unturned. So it was decided that Olivia would continue to be her primary caregiver since she was doing this for such a long time; it is only logical that she continued doing so. Grace and I were about to leave at the end of the week and for some reason we were feeling optimistic that everything was going to be alright. Naturally, there was nothing we could do in the sense of her health, but allow her to live her life in a comfortable and decent manner.

The night before we left, I decided to spend the night beside Charolette and lay on her bed. While we were there, the conversation was so rich in love and thankfulness that at one point when I looked at the clock on the wall it was already 2:30 in the morning. We were laying there reminiscing on the goodness of God and what he had done in the life of Charolette and her children.

Charolette was a little more serious when she talked about Washington. I got to hear some of the stories that had not been told to anyone before that night on the bed. I was just taking in every bit of information like a sponge. My mind was saturated with good things and the memories I was left with were good ones.

The Silent Hurt of Charolette Erica Atwell

In the morning when I woke up, I was filled with joy and I guess it was obvious because Olivia asked, "Why you seem so elated as if you've been awarded some gift of some sort?" I had not realized that whatever Charolette and I had discussed would have such an impact on my demeanor. I pulled Olivia aside and was able to share with her some of the things Charolette and I reminisced about the night before. Olivia had this big grin on her face; apparently these were things she had never heard before.

Grace and I returned home feeling good knowing that we had done everything that was required of a son, and especially knowing the tumultuous relationship they had before was now a thing of the past. After we had settled in on our arrival back in the US, we called just to let them know we had arrived home safely and were just exhausted from the flight. We kept in touch by calling home at least two or three times per week, just to check and see how Charolette was doing or if there was anything that needed attention right away in terms of Charolette's care.

That continued religiously for about three years. We would call sometimes and Charolette would not be in the best of moods or Olivia would explain:

"Some days are better than some. She has those when everything I do is wrong and Charolette just gets angry at the drop of a hat."

The beautiful thing was that Olivia would laugh it off and say she understood this was a difficult period in Charlotte's life. Charolette had become extremely ill with all kind of flu-like symptoms and joint pain. Some parts of her body were breaking out in sores. Charolette's body was wracked with pain and anxiety; her immune system

The Silent Hurt of Charolette Erica Atwell

was breaking down at a rapid pace. I remember Olivia calling me one Friday evening and saying:

"Richard, I don't think Charolette is going to make it because she is getting from bad to worse. The first thing in the morning I am going to take her the hospital to make sure because I don't like how she is looking. She has this pale look on her skin."

"I'll go to the remittance service right now and send money so you can at least have some money to process whatever you need such as medication and car fare."

In the mid-afternoon, Olivia called me and let me know the hospital was going to admit Charolette because she had a high fever and they needed to run some tests to be certain it was not anything serious or detrimental to her health. Charolette was admitted to the hospital for the next two months. At one point she was on a mechanical respirator in order to help her breathe. I said to myself, "My Lord, how much more can she take? With all of that she has gone through or going through, how can this even be possible for one human being to be suffering in such Silent Hurt and going through a lifetime of Challenges?"

I called her Primary Care Physician to ask him what Charolette's chances of surviving this illness were. He responded promptly and told me the chances were extremely small and he would be surprised if Charolette lived through this battle.

Everything came crashing down; even though we know death is inevitable, we sometimes lose the courage to accept the inescapable that we all have to go. Charolette had made up her mind and had accepted the truth that her life was coming towards the end and nothing could

The Silent Hurt of Charolette Erica Atwell

separate her from accepting her destiny. That part of her story I had not shared with anyone. I felt it wasn't significant to mention that part of the conversation to anyone, because deep down in my heart it was between Charolette and her God to decide if she lived or died.

One Sunday afternoon, the kids and I had returned from church and were sitting in the basement playing as we always did. The phone rang but I didn't answer it. It kept on ringing and ringing but I continued to ignore it, enjoying the moments I could spend with my children on a Sunday afternoon before the noise of the weekday activities took over.

"Dad, are you going to answer the phone?" my son said.

"If it rings again, I'll certainly answer," I promised.

Before I could finish that sentence the phone rang again. My heart did a little leap. I got the feeling that this was not just anyone calling for no apparent reason. When I put the receiver to my ear, I heard this deep wailing and then it struck me.

Charolette had finally reached the end of her journey; a life lived with many obstacles, stumbling blocks, mountains and valleys. In our conversation, she had asked us not to make any big fuss and carry on as if her life was in vain, but to celebrate the good things that she stood for, even in the face of adversities.

That Sunday evening, I couldn't even comprehend what Olivia was saying because she was so hysterical and I was in a different time and space. I started to cry; my kids got real emotional, looks of concern on their faces.

"What is wrong daddy?"

The Silent Hurt of Charolette Erica Atwell

"My mother died," I said simply amidst my tears.

They both hugged me tightly and assured me it was going to be alright. Grace had returned from shopping that evening a little late, but was informed by the kids of the tragedy that had occurred in my life. After that, the house phone began to ring repeatedly. Family and friends were calling from every corner of the globe expressing their condolences and offering words of compassion and kindness. I was grateful. I knew my mother had done some amazing things for those she came in contact with so it wasn't as shocking to hear so many kind words from people whom I had never met or seen before.

That Sunday I was filled with anger and sadness, unsure how to react. I went into isolation for about two days. Before any funeral arrangements were made, all the relatives had to be notified in an appropriate time frame so everyone who was able to be there could be a part of the celebration. Charolette was never one who liked to be around grumpy people or those who loved to complain and find fault with everything. Her life was lived with many encounters that made Charolette strong or vulnerable.

Olivia and Jacob were taking care of the arrangements back on the island while everyone else was planning their trip home. The funeral was set for late spring in the month of June. Olivia was politically connected with the Member of Parliament for her Constituency. In essence, 'Apple never fall far from the tree'. When Grace and I arrived back on the island, it wasn't like when we had come previously for Charolette's illness; we were more in a somber mood this time.

The Silent Hurt of Charolette Erica Atwell

The ride home wasn't about sightseeing this time but a more melancholy mood. When we arrived at the house, the yard was full with people from all parts of the community. Some were there just to view the excitement while some were there showing sincere empathy for the family. The next day Grace, Olivia, and I went to get liquor and all the other stuff we needed for the repast. For the next couple of days we were just running around making the funeral arrangements.

One of the good things that happened was that one of Charolette's grandsons had obtained his funeral director's license and decided he wanted to do the funeral. Who else could have been more qualified to plan Charolette's funeral? So we left that part to him.

There were a few glitches and bumps in the road, but it wasn't anything that couldn't be resolved in real time. One of the nights while we were there discussing how Charolette would be buried in the funeral plot, some issues raised their ugly heads. Apparently, our sister Sandra wasn't too keen on having Charolette buried beside her husband. She wanted a sepulcher for Charolette and didn't care about anything else. It was so awkward that Grace had to step in and unequivocally express her disgust at the request.

Charolette was going to be buried in the family plot in the back of the yard about two hundred feet away from the house. The young men of the community had dug the grave and cleaned up some the shrubs around the burial ground. It was just wonderful feeling seeing so many people who took part in planning Charolette's funeral; everyone took their role seriously.

The Silent Hurt of Charolette Erica Atwell

On the day of the actual funeral, two huge buses showed up from the city with people whom Charolette had grown up with and some who she had done some good for along the way. Her grandson outdid himself: the hearse was a Cadillac with glass and shiny wheels. I was even surprised at all the excitement that was going on because I didn't want it to be a spectacle. That Sunday, I stood with my eldest son who was extremely angry at what was taking place.

"This is not how I want to remember my grandmother. Most of these people who are here is just for the ride and want to be seen," he commented.

During the funeral service, all the family who were there made their speeches. Two of her dear friends were there; both gave emotional speeches about Charolette's life. This brought tears to the eyes of the many that were in attendance. Her brother Paul reminded us of her childhood how Charolette was kind and obedient to her parents. While everyone was out playing and doing other things, Charolette would remain close to her mother, absorbing everything she could learn.

The funeral wasn't long. The preacher seemed in a hurry to go for some reason; he seemed very scared and nervous. After we took Charolette to her final resting place, it was time for the wake. What surprised me was it was more like a celebration or party, if you will. There were all kinds of meat and liquor, and the music was blasting; everyone was in a festive mood. At one point, there was a little tension between some of the family members, who were arguing over all kinds of stupid things. I guess this happens a lot at funerals because no one seemed surprised. There was so much food and everybody was enjoying themselves despite the somber nature of the occasion.

I stood there reflecting on Charolette's life. My thoughts ran far away. How can people be so nonchalant? Charolette hadn't gone down in the grave for a long time and it definitely seemed like everyone had already forgotten about her. I was very troubled in my spirit. I leaned over to my son and whispered in his ears, "This is not right." He responded by saying "I know. I share the same sentiment." Some might see it as a celebration of life; but somehow, in my mind, it was more of what one can get from the deceased's family. Well the celebration carried on into the wee hours of the morning. People were drunk and passed out in different places and positions.

That night, we headed back to the city, travelling with my son, his mother, and her driver. Nothing much was said, but I knew deep down in my heart I missed Charolette so much. I guess at that time the full impact of her death hit me. Charolette had left a legacy of commitment to her family and friends and now there was no one to actually carry on the tradition. In my estimation, I didn't see anyone within the family structure who would take on that role and that included me.

The following day, there was a huge argument over Charolette's pension and whatever was left from her years of hard work. I couldn't understand what the fuss was about. I knew Charolette had given her all. Every penny that she ever earned went back into her family.

After all was said and done, the house that Charolette was living in had been purchased by her son Jacob and that is where Olivia was living also. Olivia had lived there for the period of time Charolette was ill and needed personal attention. Three months later Olivia received a notice from the lawyer that she was to vacate the premises within two months. Olivia's worst fears had come to reality. Olivia was devastated and emotionally drained from the prospect of knowing she had to leave. There was no other alternative, but to go back in the rough neighborhood she had left behind. That was more heart wrenching and painstaking going back to an environment that wasn't conducive to what she had started to experience.

Anyhow, Olivia held her head high and eventually moved out within the time frame she was told to. With a lot of resentment and hostility towards her relative, Olivia went into deep depression. I called my brother to ask him if all of this was necessary. He was extremely combative in trying to justify his actions. I was deeply hurt inside; seeing Olivia in this predicament brought a lot of anger towards my brother. How can one be so callous in watching people hurt and not show some form of empathy?

The house is still empty with no one living there, just shrubs and peeling paints all over. The yard is overrun with animals and currently in a dilapidated condition. Olivia was able to come to terms with the reality of living back in her old neighborhood. As much as she would like to be living in a more affluent community, the powers that be would not allow her. There was so much animosity between the families, Charolette would be most disappointed and hurt to see all that's going on.

I can say with a degree of certainty that my family has gone through or is going through a situation and we really never discussed as a family the long deep rooted anger and betrayal that has been so prevalent in this family.

The Silent Hurt of Charolette Erica Atwell

Years after Charolette's death, her tomb was built. Even that was an issue. I received a call from one of my nephews that he was on his way down from Europe to build the tomb for Charolette and needed me to assist financially. I was taken aback to see his total disregard for the rest of the family. I'm not saying it should not be done; but I think decisions like this need family support. It was utterly inappropriate to go ahead and do something with such self- centeredness and not allowing other family members to be a part of the planning.

For me and Olivia, it was personal because Washington, our father, was also buried there right beside his wife and the mere fact that the building of the tomb would only be about Charolette, I was totally opposed to what was going to be done. In my mind, if we were going to pursue such actions, the whole thing should have been about Charolette and Washington, not only just doing it for one. Anyhow my opinion didn't matter. The headstone was erected without Olivia's approval or mine. That painful experience brought on a lot hurt.

Olivia and I had agreed that we would take on the challenge of correcting the wrong in terms of getting a proper headstone for our father Washington. The next year, I made all the necessary plans to erect the headstone. Olivia wasn't working and her current financial situation wouldn't allow her to contribute financially so I took on the financial aspect of getting it done.

On the day it was done, Olivia and I made plans for our children and grandchildren to be a part of the planning to complete what was left undone. I am absolutely sure that our family crisis was not an isolated one or even different from other families who are struggling with the same

The Silent Hurt of Charolette Erica Atwell

dynamics of family going through this dreaded "Silent Hurt".

Family should be united and have one common goal; but I knew that would be probably a far-fetched idea. We all have our idiosyncrasies as family with different traits and experiences; we are who we are, whether we like it or not. My hope is that the legacy of Charolette would never die. Somehow, it would live on through Olivia; she has that kind compassionate way about her that I would certainly hope she would take the baton and run with it.

Growing up, unfortunately, does not protect us from vulnerability to the fears of things that happen within our scope of directions and/or phases in our lives. In fact, we are most severely and intensely affected and overwhelmed by fundamental fears from the past when they are resuscitated and materialize in unexpected events in the moments when we are challenged by our fears. We are most terrified when internal threats and real external dangers converge within our thought process. For children and adults alike, traumatic situations are analogous to earlier times in our lives when we had no words for what we going through. Our worst fears and when our cognitive resources were not yet up to the task of initiating and making sense of complex experiences within the confines of our environment. It is hard to fathom how one can be so dedicated to making all the necessary effort to keep the family together even through hardship and neglect.

So, when we look at each from the perspective of family and commitment, I sincerely, hope we're taking the obligatory steps to see each other as human beings and not just as objects. While children and adults share many of the disorganizing effects of trauma, the adult capacity to adapt

The Silent Hurt of Charolette Erica Atwell

can be sometimes challenging and hard to adapt to the fundamentals of being in a disorganized and dysfunctional family. We ought to figure out our defensive strategies, and call on internal resources. There can be a vast number of options which may include counselling from trained professional or clinical experts. In this twenty first century, the resources are vastly different from what was available to our children or when we were growing up.

Moreover, the self-protective mechanisms that they acquire through normal development are especially vulnerable to traumatic disruptions. A child's experience of helpless surrender to overwhelming circumstances threatens a multitude of problems. Until all of this occurred with the death of Charolette and seeing the kind of self -centered behavior, I never realized I had all of this resentment toward my siblings that weren't addressed at an early age.

Washington would be disappointed in me if he was here. Charolette would be in tears trying to make me understand the value of family. Even though our lives are intertwined because we share our parents, what good does it do to have only anger and resentment to each other? On the strength of Charolette and Washington, it is absolutely significant that in order for me to move on, I would have to let go of all these resentment to siblings.

Ephesians 4:29-32:

> Do not let any unwholesome talk come out of your mouths, but only what is helpful for building others up according to their needs, that it may benefit those who listen. And do not grieve the Holy Spirit of God, with whom you were sealed for the day of redemption. Get rid of all bitterness, rage and anger, brawling and slander,

along with every form of malice. Be kind and compassionate to one another, forgiving each other, just as in Christ God forgave you.

This passage of scripture has helped me immensely to learn to let go and understand the whole truth of harboring bitterness and anger. Charolette, may I someday come to the realization that what you've sown in the life you have lived may be a part of my future. Learning to love as you have loved, learning to give as you have given, words of encouragement when there is doubt, a prayer when there is nothing else that can help, and compassion when there is contempt. Charolette Erica Atwell may your soul rest in peace. You have left a lifelong lesson to all of us to love and care for those who are around you, whether family, friends, or strangers.

About the author

Ranston Ray Foster

Ranston Ray Foster was born on the island of Jamaica. Growing up in Kingston 13 at 17A Bowens Road was a period filled with a lot of challenges for young Ranston. In the mid-seventies, things became extremely difficult across the island because of political unrest and many families were disrupted. During that period, Ranston's parents decided that the best thing for the family was to move to Spanish Town, St. Catherine. Life did not change much for the family. However, it serves as a backdrop for his debut novel *The Silent Hurt of Charolette Erica Atwell*. Ranston later migrated to the United States where he currently resides.

The Silent Hurt of Charolette Erica Atwell

Proof

Made in the USA
Charleston, SC
29 January 2016